SEEᴋᴇʀ

Annika Kim – Jeff Rogers

- **EECA** -
English Educator's Cooperative Association

Seeker...

EECA - English Educator's Cooperative Association
IEK - iExperienceKorea

Book Website
www.iexperiencekorea.com

Email: jeff@iexperiencekorea.com

Give feedback on the book at:

jeff@iexperiencekorea.com
akcat1223@gmail.com

Printed in Korea

Dedicated to all cat lovers.

Prologue

I started my life in a warm soft blanket with my six brothers and sisters. Life was good. Every time I meowed milk would come right away. My mother would wash me, and feed me, and make me feel safe and secure.

We lived in the countryside with a small family beside a cool river. There were four people who lived there with us. Raymond was the father. He was a gentle, strong man who loved his family. He loved us too because he considered us part of his family. His wife's name was Elizabeth, but he just called her Beth. She was almost like a second mother to us when we were all kittens. Then there was my favorite, Terrah. She was only ten when we were born, and she loved all of us, but she loved me the most.

When we were old enough to eat solid food, Raymond made Terrah choose one of us to stay because he said we had too many cats around. Terrah was sad, but I was happy because she chose me, and all my brother and sisters went to good homes. Beth made sure of that.

Life was not perfect though, even back then. Regi was Terrah's brother. He was a year younger than Terrah, and he was an all together different kind of person. I have often wondered how a wonderful family could have such a monster as the youngest member. Regi was a monster, and so was his dog.

The dog's name was PeeBody. Regi had named him that when PeeBody was young, because he would roll over on his back and then pee all over himself. It was one of the most undignified acts I have ever seen. That was when I realized that there were irreconcilable differences between cats and dogs. I have to admit, I became quite prejudice early on in my life. I would learn later that not all dogs are bad.

I remember one event that typifies the relationship between Terrah and me. It was a cool evening and we were outside together, sitting beside the small river that ran through the back yard of our house. It was not quite dark yet, but we could see the lights inside the house, and Terrah's mother preparing dinner.

Terrah was reading me a story about a guy who ran away from home. I was so focused on the story that I didn't notice Regi and PeeBody sneaking up on us.

I jumped and hissed in surprise as PeeBody gave a loud bark close to my ear. Then, he opened his enormous jaws and revealed his fangs. With a sudden jolt, I realized he was going to bite me. I let out a fearful screech and tried to dodge the dog's mouth. PeeBody's jaws snapped at end of my tail and I jumped forward. He missed me, but I fell into the swirling icy water.

I am not a good swimmer, and cats hate to swim, so I dunked under and swallowed a huge mouth full of water. I came up sputtering and gasping for breath, but quickly went under again because the river was too deep, and I couldn't feel the ground with my feet. I started to panic, and my short life flashed before my eyes. I tried to cry out for help, but only got another mouth full of water. I felt sure I was going to die. I was getting so breathless, and was about to give up when someone splashed violently into the water near me. It was Terrah.

Terrah's hand grabbed me by the fur. She lifted me, and I clung onto her shoulder with thorn sharp claws. I suddenly felt safe and began to relax just a little.

She carried me to the shore but she didn't put me down because she could feel my body shivering with cold. Water dropped down from her clothes and I could feel that she was cold too. I coughed a lung full of river water onto her shoulder, but she didn't mind. Regi and PeeBody ran off snickering and howling while Terrah glared at them until they disappeared. I would have hissed myself, but I still couldn't breathe very well.

"It's all okay now, Kitty." Terrah soothed me. She always called me Kitty and I liked it. I guess I knew it wasn't a real name, but that didn't matter.

That is only half the story of our special friendship, however. One day when

Terrah came home from school, I found her outside, trapped in the corner between the house and the garage. There was a huge rat there, with red eyes and long yellow teeth that were dripping with saliva.

Terrah had always been especially afraid of rats, but fortunately, I wasn't, and I came to her rescue. I dashed heroically between Terrah and the rat. We faced each other, and that rat was nearly as big as me. I hissed at him, and jumped squarely on his back, digging my sharp claws into his shoulders as I bit his left ear, tearing it in half. The rat gave out a squeak of pain and surprise. He tired to run away, but I held him tightly and punished him until I felt certain that he would never bother Terrah again.

Chapter 1

One fine day I was sleeping in the window behind the sofa. The warm sunshine beamed into my fur making me lazy. Then suddenly, there was a loud noise, and I jumped in surprise. It was Raymond slamming the door as he came home from work, but as I looked up at him, I could see that there was something different about him. He seemed very happy and excited.

I went over to greet him, rubbing myself on his chubby leg and purring. He scooped me up and nuzzled me with his nose, carrying me to the kitchen and laughing. Terrah was helping Elizabeth cook, and PeeBody was begging for crumbs. I jumped from Raymond's arms, sailed over PeeBody, and landed on the sofa.

"You guys are never going to believe what happed today.", he told them. Terrah and Beth looked at him curiously and waited for him to continue. He went on. "I got a big promotion, and that means we are going to have a lot more money!"

There was a long moment of silence as they looked at him with open mouths. "You're kidding!" Beth finally said.

"No. I'm serious!" Raymond answered. "They want me to manage the New York branch of the company."

"No way!" Terrah shouted. "We are moving to New York?" I didn't understand what they were talking about, but it was obviously big news, and everyone was excited, even PeeBody.

Suddenly, Regi, who was passing by in the hallway, stuck his head in the doorway and said, "New York! Whoa pop! That's rad!" Then he walked over to PeeBody and started rubbing his belly. "Did you hear that, boy?" he said. "We're going to New York." But PeeBody just stuck his huge tongue out and wagged his tail in the stupid way that dogs do.

Terrah had come over to me, wiping her hands on her apron. She sat on the sofa next to me and put me on her lap, talking softly to me, explaining something. But I just enjoyed her warm breath in my face and purred in response, letting her know that I shared her excitement, even though I didn't know exactly what all of this meant.

Terrah had this smell, like sweet apples, and I took big breaths into my nostrils, enjoying the love that I felt for her. If she was happy, then I was happy too.

The next week was a crazy blur of activity and disruption. Everything was picked up and put into boxes. It was rather upsetting at first, but Terrah and the family were having such a happy time that soon I felt ok with all the mess and confusion. I began to understand that we were leaving and moving somewhere else, and that thought scared me a little bit even though I also felt excited about it.

Finally, the big day came, and we watched the moving truck leave our driveway. I glanced around our house for the last time. It seemed so empty and unfamiliar, and I felt empty too. But then, Terrah picked me up and hugged me, which made everything feel better.

She carried me to our van and climbed into the back seat. I sat on her lap, feeling warm and cozy, and snuggled down even more closely with a deep contented purr. She rubbed behind my ear until I fell asleep.

I don't know how long I slept, but I woke up to the sound of music. Raymond, Beth, and Terrah were singing *'100 Bottles of Beer on the Wall'*. Regi was sitting in the back with a dis-intrigued look on his face, and PeeBody lay beside him, resting his chin on his paws. They both looked bored. Regi dug his headphones out of his navy backpack and put them on.

We traveled on about 30 minutes more, and then Raymond turned the van into a rest area beside some small town, and we stopped.

I stood up and looked out the window, but Terrah pulled me back down. She held me in the van while the rest of the family got out. PeeBody had a leash, and he walked proudly beside Regi as I sadly watched them all disappear together behind a row of cars. I wanted to follow them, but I couldn't figure out how to get out of the van.

I looked around in desperation, feeling lonely and left behind. But then, I felt a soft breeze of fresh air ripple my fur. I turned to see that Raymond's door was slightly opened. So I snaked my way to the front and pushed against the door with my head. It opened easily and I leaped gracefully to the pavement, excited to explore this new place and to find Terrah.

I had never been to a parking lot before and I didn't know what to expect. I let out a hiss of surprise and fluffed out my fur as a bright red car zoomed past me, almost hitting my tail. Forgetting everything in my panic to get out of the road, I ducked under a parked car. In my experience, parked cars were always a safe place to hide.

This time though, the thundering sound of the powerful engine roared in my ears, and I quickly changed my mind. I ran out from under the car, my amber eyes wide in fear, and darted toward a group of garbage cans on the sidewalk, slipping between two of them, using them for a place to hide. I gasped to catch my breath and wished now that I would have stayed in the car. Just then, a familiar smell of sweet apples caught my nose.

I would know that smell anywhere, and my ears pricked up in hope and relief. Forgetting my fear and anxiety, I lifted my nose to the air and began tracking the wonderful smell of my Terrah. It was coming from the left of me, where it seemed like hundreds of people were swarming over the sidewalk, going to and from the restrooms. I went in that direction, trying to pick out Terrah's face among crowd. But soon I realized that the direction of Terrah's scent was changing, moving back toward the parking lot, and leading me back there.

The happy prospect of rejoining Terrah again overcame my fear of that dangerous place, and I leaped off the curb onto the pavement, following my nose. I was looking for our van, and it only took me a few moments to spot it. I started running toward it in relief and excitement, but my happiness turned to fear and confusion as I saw it began to slowly move away, gradually gaining speed. With panicked yowl of dismay, I streaked after it, hard on my paws, grinding them raw on the hot pavement.

For a moment I thought I might catch up. I was just behind the van. I might be close enough, so I closed my eyes and took a mighty leap toward the bumper. It was my last chance, but I failed. My paws hit the bumper's edge, and pain scorched through my small outstretched body. I unsheathed my claws, trying to cling onto the bumper, but they slipped off the cold metal and I fell to the ground, coughing in the black smoke from the exhaust.

Everything was hazy and I felt as though I might black out. Through squinting eyes I caught a glimpse of our van getting farther and farther away until it finally disappeared from my sight. I tried to get up to chase after it again, but something was preventing me from moving. I suddenly felt so tired, and I closed my eyes for a moment, allowing myself to focus on my pain.

Something was wrong with my front leg. It must have been hurt when I hit the bumper, and the pain of it made my head swim. Just then, a giant truck roared past me, picking up speed.

That was too much for me, and I realized that I had to get out of the street. I gathered all the strength I could and dragged myself toward the grassy margin to the right of the driveway.

My leg wouldn't cooperate, so I had to drag it painfully beside me. It hurt so badly that I didn't think I could make it, but somehow I did. I gasped for air, and when I finally arrived safely at the edge of the road, I let myself go limp. Right there beside the roaring cars and trucks, I completely blacked out.

Chapter 2

When I finally blinked open my eyes, I was lying on my side in the grass. At first I thought I was sitting in our old backyard, until I saw the road. For a minute, I had no idea where I was, or why. But then the sharp pain in my leg reminded me, and the horrible experiences of the day came rushing back into my mind. I closed my eyes again, wishing all of this was just a horrible nightmare. But when I opened them hopefully once more, it was no use. I wanted to wail out loud.

It was getting pretty dark, so I figured it must be late; way past my usual dinner time, and along with my pain and fear, my belly also was growling with hunger. I thought of the warm food and comfortable kitchen at our old house. '*Terrah...*' I thought to myself. '*Why did we have to leave.*' I felt a pang of homesickness stab me like a knife through my heart. It hurt even more than my leg.

I had to start moving because this was a very dangerous place, and I knew I needed to get out of there if I wanted to survive. The first problem was my leg. I pulled myself up, balancing on three legs, testing to see if my injured leg was broken. If it was, it would be really bad. Gingerly, I put my bad front foot on the grass and let a little of my weight rest on it. It hurt a lot, but it didn't seem to be broken, since it supported that little bit of weight. I let out a sigh, half in pain and half in relief, and sat down for a moment to collect myself and look around.

There was a building that smelled of delicious food nearby on the other side of a fence. Light was beaming out of the front doors, and people swarmed in and out. I licked my lips. That place definitely had food.

With some confidence, I felt that I could act cute and beg the people for something to eat. I let out a throaty purr at the thought of food. Terrah would come back for me, and I could fill my belly while I waited. The thought that I could see her again made my heart swell, giving me comfort and strength. I limped forward and made my way slowly toward the front door of the building. Thankfully, it was in the direction AWAY from the road. I definitely wanted to avoid the cars.

The main door was open because it was a warm summer night, and I easily slipped through, eager to get some help and some food. The delicious mouth watering smell was getting stronger, and I forgot all my fear, padding forward through the door.

I zeroed in on a lady walking toward me with something that smelled of fish in her hands. I meowed to get her attention, but she still didn't see me. If she was like Terrah, she'd give me some food for sure. I limped forward, trying to look as helpless as possible, and rubbed myself confidently at her legs. But then, something I didn't expect happened.

She let out a screech of surprise and started kicking, but at the same time, she dropped what she was holding. Frustration bubbled up in my belly. It was completely unnecessary to kick me. It was so offensive! But my outrage quickly changed to fear as one of her legs hit my shoulder, spinning my body around so that I landed painfully on my bad leg. I let out a hiss of pain and tried to run away.

But then, I saw a giant piece of fish that had fallen from her hands. I grabbed the huge chunk in my mouth and started to scurry back out, but she kicked me one final time, and I flew out the door still holding my supper. When I landed, I sprinted away, ears back with my tail flying behind me.

I was still in shock. How could a human be so mean? Evan Regi wouldn't kick me like that. I ran around the corner into a narrow alley, looking for dark place to eat my fish. In the very corner, behind a box, I found a spot where I thought I could eat in peace. I settled down and was just about to take a huge, hungry bite, when something furry moved in the corner of my eye.

I had already suffered a lot, and I couldn't imagine what was going to happen to me now. I spun around hissing, and was very surprised at what I saw. It was a dog.

He was looking at my fish, and there was no way I was going to give it up to a dirty dog. I had already fought too hard for it, and I would fight him too if I had too. I crouched down, ignoring the pain in my leg, and pushed my fish behind me with my good paw. A growl rumbled deep in my chest, and I examined my opponent, looking for any weakness.

It was an old brown hound dog with grey fur on his muzzle, sprinkling his nose and mouth with a salty complexion. His coat was dirty, and he was really thin; almost starved. His eyes had that hazy look of an old dog that was losing his sight, and the way he looked at me was a surprise.

I had half expected him to attack me, but there was a curious amusement in his gaze instead. He started to move, and I crouched lower, ready to fight, but he didn't come any closer. Instead, he just sat down with a grunt and held me with that same look. We sat that

that way for a minute, just looking each other over until he finally spoke with a deep, husky voice.

"I saw you..." he began "...with that fish. You did it the hard way. There are much easier ways to get food."

I looked back at him doubtfully."You don't look so good at getting food." I told him, challengingly. "You are skin and bones. Why are you bothering me. Just go away and leave me alone unless you want a bloody nose."

He laughed at me, but not unkindly. "You talk tough, but you are a pet, aren't you?" he was watching me knowingly. "I've seen your kind many times, and you won't last a week on your own. You'll get hit by a car or starve to death before long."

I gulped, trying to keep my composure. "I don't need your advice." I told him. "My girl will come back for me. I just have to wait for her."

The dog snorted. "You really believe that, don't you?" he said, and then carried on without waiting for an answer. "I used to think that too, when I was young. But it never happened. You're the same as me. You're abandoned, my boy. You'll just have to survive on your own for now."

I felt my blood turn to ice. Would Terrah have abandoned me? No! Terrah wouldn't do that. It was my fault that I didn't stay in the car. But still, a small voice in my head said, *'But why did she leave you?'* I pushed the thought violently away, and tried to convince myself. She must have forgotten me, but not on purpose. Still though, uncertainty clung to my mind like a growing shadow.

The old dog stared at me, then continued talking. "My name is Skipper. Getting food from humans directly isn't the smartest way to survive."

I stared at him blankly, but he didn't seem to notice the conflict going on inside me. Skipper continued. "I know a place where humans store their food. The window is always open, but I'm too big to get inside." He eyed me up and down. "But you... you can easily do it. If you join me, I can teach you how to live a good life." he watched me, waiting for an answer.

Rage and grief choked me, and I didn't say anything right away. I already had a good life. How dare Skipper suggest a better life then the one I lived with Terrah?

"No" I snapped, emotional agony twisting my face into a frown or sorrow. "I can survive alone until Terrah notices I'm gone, and comes to find me." I whipped around and raced away. I didn't want to talk, especially to a stupid, stranger dog. Besides, big wet tears were rolling down my face.

Chapter 3

I spent a sleepless night under a small bridge, shivering in the cold night air. For a long time my fear and sadness kept me awake, but I finally fell into a fitful sleep just around dawn.

The sun was shining down on my fur when I finally woke up, late in the morning. The penetrating warmth felt good, and for a moment I imagined I was back home, sitting in the window. Then I blinked the sleep from my eyes, and felt a rock in the pit of my stomach as I remembered everything from the day before.

My belly grumbled like it had never done before. I was so hungry, and couldn't believe I had left my hard won fish behind when I ran away from Skipper. I should have grabbed it when I ran, but I was so upset then.

I closed my eyes again, wishing all of this was a terrible nightmare; a dream where we never moved, a dream where I never jumped out of the car, and a dream where I never met Skipper. But when I opened eyes, the truth of my situation came crashing down on me once more. My belly grumbled again, and I wished my food bowl was right in front of me. Terrah always fed me soft, canned cat food in the morning, and my mouth watered at the thought. I had to do something.

What options did I have? I remembered what Skipper told me, and for a moment, I thought about joining up with him. But I still had too much pride to go crawling back. There was no way I was going to risk my life again by going back to the food court. That was almost a total disaster the first time. I heard from my mother about stray cats that ate from garbage cans, but I didn't think I would ever be ready for that. Finally, I decided to just scout around looking for opportunities because I didn't have any better plan.

My leg was starting to feel a bit better, so I figured I would just sniff around a bit to see if there was any food that humans had dropped. I circled the building where the food court was and did find a couple of scraps, but it wasn't enough to fill my belly, and it only made me even more hungry.

After a while I gave up, made my way dejectedly back to my secret place under the bridge, and flopped down exhausted. I was very hungry, and in a thoroughly bad mood. As I lay there, I noticed something flash past my eye, and I leaped up to see what it was.

It was a small beetle, and surprisingly, my belly roared at the sight of it. I jumped up, and batted it down with my good paw, trapping it in the grass. Without thinking I grabbed it in my mouth and bit it. It made a big crunching sound and squirted bug guts all inside my mouth. It gagged me and I tried to spit it out. I sputtered at the taste and gagged some more to get it out of my mouth. I hurried down to the river that flowed slowly under the bridge. Stooping down, I lowered my muzzle to the water to get a long drink and wash out the horrible taste.

The water was nice and cool. I was still drinking, when I saw a movement in the water. It was a small golden fish. My mouth watered at the sight, and all my instincts told me to catch it and eat it. I went into my hunting stance. My paw shot out like lighting in an attempt to scoop it out of the water, but I failed. The fish was almost as fast as me, and the prey was slippery too, so catching it turned out to be harder than I had thought. I tried many times, but had to wait between attempts because all the fish ran away and wouldn't return for a while. Frustration bubbled up in my throat and I felt like yowling.

More than three hours passed, and the sun was high it the sky. Concentrating so hard and working in the hot sun had made my hunger critical now. I couldn't keep doing this, and a desperate thought in the back of my mind began to creep forward. There may be no choice me but to go crawling back to Skipper. It might be the only way for me to survive until Terrah came back for me.

'Why didn't she come?' I thought, beginning to feel the first little twinge of anger and doubt toward her. But I quickly moved my mind away from that painful line of thought. With my tail between my legs and my head hanging low, I began my search for Skipper.

I had a pretty good idea where to find him; there in that dark alley where we had first met. Believe it or not, that was where I found him, sitting there patiently and peacefully, staring into the sky, watching the clouds go by. I stood there for a moment some distance away, just watching him and wondering how he could have survived this long without regular food.

As I stirred, my foot accidently landed on a dry leaf and the sound of it reminded me of the sound when I bit into the beetle. I shoved that disgusting thought out of my mind as Skipper turned his attention toward me. He smiled smugly, and said in his raspy dog voice, "I thought you would come sooner."

Embarrassment rippled my fur, making the hair on my back stand up. '*How dare he say that!?*' I thought to myself. But I didn't want the old dog to think I could be easily upset by his words, so I calmed my voice, flattened my fur, and answered in a clear, confident voice that echoed in the alley. "Yes, I came back."

The old dog seemed taken aback at the authority in my voice, and for a moment he was silent. He looked me over, as if sizing me up all over again. I felt a twinge of satisfaction, and as the dog snorted, I got straight to business. "I didn't come back because I was desperate." I lied. "I felt pity for you, and decided to help you. So what should I do?"

Skipper snorted at me again, a mocking smile curling the corners of his lips. "I know you're lying Kiddo. No one has felt pity for me in a long time." he said laughing. "But since you agree, we'll go and see what you can get."

I snorted this time, trying to maintain my composure at his mocking tone. "Ok. You know more about this place than I do, so where is the food?" I growled at him. My hunger was making me impatient, and I didn't like dogs anyway.

"I know where the food is." Skipper replied. "I'll take you there tonight."

I tried to argue, but Skipper cut me off and started talking again. He explained, "In the daytime, humans are always around, but they go home after dark, so we have to wait or they will catch us." he said simply.

Anger and hungry impatience bubbled together in my belly. "Fine." I growled, trying not to let him see my desperation. "I'll be back later." I turned to go, but had not taken more than three steps when Skipper's raspy voice came to me once again.

"You should take your fish." he said. "I am tired of watching it for you." I turned to look at him, but he had already turned around and was walking away, his back toward me.

I looked over to the box where I had left the fish the day before. Sure enough, there it was, right where I had left it, untouched and uneaten. I didn't know what to say, and I have to admit that I was pretty flustered. The only dog I had ever really known was PeeBody, and he was so greedy that there was no way he ever would have resisted eating my fish.

"You don't have to thank me." Skipper said over his shoulder, without stopping or looking back. "I felt a little pity for you, that's all." I could hear him chuckling to himself as he walked away, and my eyes followed his thin figure until he disappeared around the corner.

Only a moment before, I would have felt insulted and angry to hear him laughing quietly like that. But now, I felt a mixture of gratefulness and confusion. He was so skinny, and I was still quite plump. I knew he was hungrier than I was. I felt a little bit ashamed of myself, but that awkward feeling soon evaporated into thin air as I approached my beautiful fish, my sweet fish, my delicious, hard won, wonderful fish.

It had been warm the day before when I had left it there, and it was cold now, but I didn't care. I took it in my teeth, holding one side of it down with my paw, and I took a good sized bite, tearing the soft meat away, chewing it savoringly, enjoying every second. But while I was eating, the thought of Skipper invaded my mind, interrupting my enjoyment.

My eyes had been closed, but I opened them and stopped chewing for a moment, looking over my shoulder, actually feeling like Skipper might be watching me, but he wasn't. I turned back to my fish, swallowed the first mouthful, and took another wonderful bite. As I tried to enjoy it, the same thing happened again. I realized that I was feeling guilty, and I wouldn't be able to enjoy my meal with that feeling always hanging over my head, so I sat down to think.

After a long pause, I made up my mind. I leaned forward again, tore my precious fish in half, and set one half of it aside for Skipper. Feeling much better, I happily finished off my half of the fish, and then settled down to wait, guarding Skipper's fish until he returned.

****

I had accidently fallen asleep, and when I opened my eyes, It was already dusk. I scrambled to my paws and stretched, then looked around anxiously wondering if Skipper was here yet.

My eyes scanned the ally, and landed on Skipper who was watching my every move. "Awake yet?" he said, amusement sparkling in his eyes.

Before that would've embarrassed me, but now I found myself laughing along. I thought I understood Skipper better now. I suddenly wondered if he had eaten the fish, and looked to where I had left it. It was still there, untouched. "You can eat that, you know." I said.

"I know." he said matter of factly. "I could have eaten it yesterday, but I saved it for you. I don't want to take it back again."

"Oh." I said softly, feeling a little uncomfortable about it. I couldn't eat it in front of him, and I couldn't just throw it away either. "How about if we share it?"

Skipper hesitated for a moment, watching me, which made me even more uncomfortable. But then he stood and walked over. "Ok." he said, sitting down by the fish with a grunt and pulling the piece of meat apart with his claws. "This is your half, and this is mine."

We ate in silence. When I looked up at Skipper, I was surprised to see the inside of his mouth when he chewed. He was missing a lot of teeth, but still he was eating with rapid bites, and his fish was gone in a second. Dogs always ate fast.

"Come on." he mumbled, licking his lips and turning away. "We're wasting moonlight."

I had wanted to eat my fish slowly, but I gulped it down like a dog. "

'*When in Rome...*' I thought to myself, and padded after him. We walked along for a while, passing some closed businesses. There were a few people around, but not many, and they ignored us. We finally entered into a warehouse area, and Skipper turned into a parking lot that had a long, low building in it. "This is the place." he rasped.

Feeling a bit creepy at the look of the place, I surveyed the two windows high up, at the top of the walls. One of the windows was open, and I could faintly smell raw meat. It made my mouth water, but I sat down, licking my bad paw, trying to look cool and composed. "Is that how we get in?" I asked.

Skipper nodded, and after pausing for a moment, he asked, "Do you know how to open doors?"

"No." I said, feeling a little bit shy.

But Skipper didn't tease me. "Don't worry." he said. "You're a smart kid. I'll teach you how."

His attitude made me feel better, and I felt encouraged. "Ok." I said. "Teach me how."

Skipper pointed to the door in front of the container with his nose. "You see that handle?" he said.

I nodded, concentrating and paying close attention to everything he said.

"You can't open the round ones. You need hands for that. But this kind will open easily if you hang your weight on it. All you have to do is get in through the window." He nodded toward the open window. "Then you just have to jump up and hold onto that handle. It'll be slippery, so it might take you a couple of tries. Don't give up and you'll get it."

"Why don't we open the door from the outside?" I interrupted.

"If I could do that, I wouldn't have asked you for help." he growled, but not unkindly. "Its locked." he explained simply. "It can only be opened from the inside."

"Ahh." I nodded knowingly. "I get it. I guess I just have to get through that window." I said, looking up. it was pretty high, and my paw was hurting, but I was sure I could do it.

"What are you waiting for?" Skipper asked me. "Let's get it done."

Chapter 4

I glanced up at the window for a moment, took a deep breath, and gathered my hind legs compactly beneath me, ready to leap. With a cat's agility, I leaped powerfully, bounced once on the wall to refine my aim, and the front of my body landed perfectly in the window. Hanging there, I gathered all my strength and heaved myself upward, scrambling awkwardly with my hind legs. Finally, I found myself sitting on the windowsill, gasping for air but trying not to show it. I looked down to see Skipper nod at me in approval. I nodded back at him and then jumped down to the floor inside.

Of course, the first thing I noticed was the overpoweringly delicious smell of meat. But it was cold inside, and there was a plastic curtain between the door and the stored boxes of food. I turned away toward the door, and looked up at my next task. "Skipper." I called. "I'm in. Can you hear me?"

"Loud and clear." he answered from the other side. "Now open the door. Do just like we talked about."

"OK." I told him, and jumped up, grabbing the handle with my front paws. But I was surprised at how slippery it was, even though Skipper had warned me about it. I tried again, and couldn't seem to hold on. My injured paw was getting better, but it still hurt, and it wasn't very strong yet. I tried again and again with the same result, and felt frustration growing, tightening my chest. Finally, after about ten tries, I called out to Skipper, "I can't seem to open it. I keep slipping off. Maybe there is another way."

Skipper patiently laughed his throaty laugh, and said, "I thought cats were known for their patience. Try again! Don't give up!" he said encouragingly.

I growled with determination and got ready to try again. I jumped up and pushed my whole weight on the handle. It went down, but not enough before I slipped off and fell to the ground again. I decided to slow down and think more about what I was doing wrong. I sat down and reviewed what I've been doing in my head. I was tiring to hold the handle with both my paws on one side. Suddenly, an idea popped into my head. What if I grab the handle from both sides? It would make it harder to slip. I felt some excitement together with a strange certainty that this was going to work.

This time when I leaped into the air, time seemed to slow. I slipped my one paw under the handle, and the other paw over the top. Sure enough, I was able to hang there much longer this time, and the handle slowly began to inch downward under my weight. I was struggling to hold on, but the door finally made a clink sound and opened a little, with my body still hanging on.

Skipper pushed the door wide open with his head and blinked at me proudly. "You did well. you can let go now." He said with humor.

I nodded and dropped next to him feeling proud myself. "So shall we get the food?" I asked.

"Of course." He answered, but he was already pushing his big head through the plastic curtain. I followed him close behind and shivered. "It's really cold in here." I said. "What's up with that?" There was confusion in my voice, along with some curiosity.

"Meat goes bad if you try to save it." Skipper told me, with only half of his attention. He was nosing around inside boxes, looking for something good. "The cold makes it last longer somehow."

I was shivering, and decided to start pawing around a bit myself. But almost right away, Skipper found what he was looking for. "Jackpot!" he said, grabbing a large plastic bag from inside of a box with his teeth.

"What is it?" I asked him excitedly, my stomach growling at the thought of food.

"It'shHambuguh." he said around a mouth full of plastic.

I nodded, wondering why he chose hamburger. But I didn't ask because I didn't want to sound ignorant. Hamburger was just fine with me, although I had been hoping for some fresh fish. We had left the building, and Skipper was heading back toward the place where we had met, with me right on his tail. He paused though, and turned his head toward me. "cah oouclosh sha dooh, kid?" he asked me.

I looked at him blankly, not understanding what he said because of the plastic in his mouth. He put the hamburger down so I could understand him better. "Can you close the door, kid?"

"Why?" I asked, as I turned back to do what he said.

"We don't want the humans to know we were here." he answered kindly, waiting for me before he picked up his load and started walking again.

"Oh. So we're coming back again." I stated happily, thinking that I could do this again, much easier the next time.

Skipper nodded. "Let's go back to the ally to eat."

"Okay" I answered happily. We walked back to the ally. That's when I realized that I hadn't thought about Terrah for a long time. I felt guilty because she was my best friend in my whole life. But at the same time, I felt mad at the thought that Terrah left me alone.

I understood they could have driven away without me by mistake, but I couldn't understand why she didn't come back for me, even after two days. And Skipper's words echoed hauntingly in my mind. *'You're the same as me. You're abandoned, my boy. You'll just have to survive on your own for now.'*

The fear I had felt for my own survival was actually getting better now. I had learned many things that day, and I knew now that I could survive on my own, and even though my heart yearned for Terrah, I felt that I had grown this day and that I would be ok.

Skipper was approaching the alley, and it looked like he was heading back there for the big meal. "Hey." I said to him. "I know a better place where we can eat in peace." I had bad memories of that alley, and eating there wouldn't help my digestion. "I found a grassy place under a bridge were no one goes. Follow me." That was our first big meal together.

Chapter 5

I guess about two years had passed, because the snow had come and gone more than once, and it was in the middle of a hot summer. I tried not to think about Terrah, because when I did, I felt a mixture of sadness and anger. She had never come back for me, and I don't know when it happened, but at some point, I guess I had just stopped waiting.

I had changed a lot in that time. I had lost all of my pet fat, and I was lean and strong. I had never run away from people before, but after experiencing life as a stray cat, I had to change, because strays are not loved. People threw things at me, and tried to kick me whenever I got too close. Not everybody was like that, but on average, I found out that humans were not nearly as nice as I had always thought they were.

Skipper was getting really old. His eyes became all cloudy, and he mostly just laid around, his breath having harshly from time to time, but he still always told me what to do. I didn't mind because we had become best friends. If you had told me before that I would be best friends with a dog, I would have said you were crazy, but it wasn't crazy to me now.

It was a fine, shiny summer day, and we were lying in the grass, sunning ourselves and being lazy. "Hey Skipper." I said. "Are you hungry? I'm thinking about going for some food." I waited, but there was no answer. *'He must be sleeping.'* I thought, padding over to him to cautiously and gently prodding him. "Hey Skipper?" I whispered. "Are you hungry?" But there was still no answer.

Suddenly, there was a weird feeling in the pit of my stomach, and I felt strangely afraid. When I leaned in close, I could hear him breathing, but it was VERY slow and soft so that I had to strain to hear him. I started to panic. "SKIPPER!!" I yowled, prodding him more fiercely. He opened his big wet eyes slowly, and raised one of his white eyebrows toward me.

He spoke barely in a whisper and rasped. "I'm sorry. I don't think I'll be able to stay with you anymore."

"What do you mean?" I screeched. "What are you talking about?" In my heart I knew this day would come, but the shock was almost more than a lightning strike to my mind.

"I just want to thank you, kiddo." he told me weakly. "You've made my life a lot more fun than it used to be, and I've been happy to be your friend."

I closed my eyes and shook my head. I didn't want to hear what he was saying. His words were tearing at my heart and I felt like I was going to throw up. I couldn't even imagine what it would be like without Skipper. But he kept talking in his familiar voice.

"I'm glad you are here with me now. I always worried about dying alone." He snorted very weakly, trying to show some of his old humor, and then he closed his glistening eyes.

I had never known anyone who died, and I didn't know what to do. Of course I felt sorrow and sadness for Skipper, but I also wondered what I was going to do without him. I didn't really need him to help me survive anymore. Actually, I had been feeding both of us for quite some time now, and had become very proficient at getting food. The thing that really scared me was the fear of being alone. I had never been alone, and the thought of it sent cold shivers up my spine.

"No, Skipper." I told him, my eyes full of tears as I sat in front of his huge head. I reached up and batted his nose playfully with my paw, hoping that he would put up some energy and respond like he used to do. But he couldn't have played even if he wanted too. His breathing was in ragged gasps now, shallow and ineffective. I could see his lips turning blue, and he didn't answer me anymore.

Skipper left me alone that afternoon, and I was completely lost about what I should do. I just sat there beside him, and I didn't even count the time that passed by.

Some big black birds came, and sat in the tree, watching us. I didn't like that, and asked them to go away, but they didn't leave. Every time I looked up there, they were still sitting there, just watching us. It would have made me angry if I had not been so sad.

I think a couple of days went by, and I had fallen asleep beside Skipper's body, when a rustling noise disturbed me and I woke up to see three big blackbirds sitting on top of Skipper, pecking at his head and eyes. I hissed in anger and horror, jumping up suddenly and springing onto the one closest to me. He was as big as me, but I surprised him, and ran my sharp claws over the side of his head, scratching across is evil black eye. He let out a screech that hurt my ears, and jumped up into the air, beating his wings in my face painfully as he flew away, head turned sideways so that he could see with the one good eye he had left. I will never forget that terrifying experience, and it haunts my dreams to this very day.

I don't know how long it took for Skipper's body to start smelling bad, but a boy found us there, and must have gone and told his father about it, because the man came soon after and looked at us both laying there. I hadn't eaten in days, and I felt weak and sick. I didn't care what happened to me now, I was so depressed and sad about my friend. I was skinny and dirty, and I barely raised my head as they came closer and knelt down to examine me more carefully.

The man took a phone out of his pocket and made a call, talking into it while he stood there looking at us. Then he left, and I sank into a fog of dark dreams and haunting memories of the time Skipper and I had been together. But then, Skipper turned into Terrah, and I got confused. I drifted in and out of these strange dreams, and I had forgotten where I was and what had really happened to me.

The sound of a truck engine pulling up and stopping near the bridge broke into my consciousness enough to arouse me from my fitful sleep. It took effort to raise my head when a man in a brown uniform came crashing thought the tall grass. He had a net in his hands, and after looking at me and Skipper for a minute, he swished that net right over me and scooped me up.

Panic gave me strength, and I went wild in the net, twisting and squirming, trying to scratch and climb my way up and out, but a string had drawn it closed around me, and I only managed to completely exhaust my starved body so that I quickly collapsed, and lay there inert as he dropped me limply out onto the cold metal floor of a cage, and then locked the door. I swooned away again, and woke later to the sickly smell of medicine and disinfectant.

I was laying on my side on the cold, slippery metal floor, and for a few minutes, I couldn't remember what had happened to me. Then I heard the sound of barking dogs, and my memories came flooding back again, along with my pain. "Skipper, my friend." I thought to myself, and I cried. I never saw him again.

The roaring sound of the engine made me realize that we were still in the truck. I stared into the darkness, and as my eyes began to adjust, I saw there were many other cages around me. There was one right next to me, and I peered closely at it. Inside was a large brown tabby cat with his back toward me. "Hello?" I called to him.

He turned toward me, fixing me with his bright blue eyes. His gaze was intense and scary. "What?" he rumbled in a husky, unfriendly voice.

"Umm...Do you know where we are going?" I asked carefully.

"Of course." he growled. "This is the second time I've been captured by humans. They take you to a place called a 'pound'." He paused. "Some people call it an animal shelter, but that's a lie." he hissed.

I jumped, startled by his sinister sound. He was angry about something important. "What do they do to us there? What's a lie?" I asked again.

"At first they give you food and shelter until some humans take you to their home."

I brightened. "Isn't that good?"

No!" he hissed again. "There are too many animals, and it's a rare chance that you'll be chosen. You just sit there with false hopes, and if you're not chosen within a week..." he leaned over and whispered. "... you *die*."

I gulped, and a shiver ran through my whole body. I was going to ask him some more questions but the truck came to a stop, and shortly the door opened. I squinted my eyes against the light that flooded into the truck.

A man with hairy arms lifted my cage and pulled it out. I reached my paw out through the spaces in the bars, trying to claw him so that he would let me go, but my leg wasn't long enough to reach. He was swinging the cage, so it was hard to keep my balance.

He held the brown tabby's cage in his other hand, and the cat was hissing and spitting in outrage, his fur bristling, and hackles raised menacingly.

The man carried us into a building through a door that said "Do Not Enter." As soon as the door opened, an explosion of barking and meowing deafened my ears, and I folded them back against my head. He took us to the end of the room and opened the door of my cage.

I bolted through the sudden opening thinking that might be free, but I was wrong. It was just a bigger cage, and another door slammed shut in my face as I realized it and tried to escape. The man chuckled as he walked away. This was the first time I had ever been caged, and it was humiliating.

I sat down, feeling heavily defeated and scared. The man didn't leave, and I watched him as he opened a little terrier's cage, taking a leash and clipping it to his collar so he could lead him toward a door with a skull and bones sign on it.

The little dog shrieked and whimpered, trying to get away, but the man was too strong and the leash held him tight. "Heal, dog!" the man grunted, jerking on the leash and sending the little dog sliding across the concrete floor, barking and shrieking all the way.

That frightening door opened and closed, cutting short the dog's cries, but my cage was near the end of the row, close to the door, so I could still hear him barking faintly. After a few moments however, the pitiful barking changed to high pitched yelping, and then, even that was suddenly silenced. A few minutes later, the door opened and the man came out alone, brushing his hands together and wiping them on his pants. I never saw that little dog again.

My eyes were huge and my mouth was open, my body paralyzed as if I'd been struck by lightning. I realized that experience might happen to me next, when my week ran out.

Chapter 6

I guess two or three days passed in that horrible place, and every day, more animals were killed. I had so much stress that I could hardly eat, and all the animals were nervous, especially the ones who had been there for a while.

I had been laying there with my paws over my eyes, thinking of Terrah and Skipper, when a man with tattoos all over his left arm entered the room where we were. He looked a lot like the man who lifted my cage and killed the terrier, except he wasn't fat. He looked like a rough character, and he had a lot of muscles. The sleeves of his shirt were rolled up high to show them off.

Thomas, a skinny employee with braces and glasses, was with him. "So what kind of animal are you looking for?" Thomas asked.

"A cat." The tattoo man grunted. I pricked my ears.

"What for?" Thomas asked eyeing him up and down. I guessed it was because the man didn't look like a 'pet person'.

"I work on a cargo ship..." The man explained gruffly without looking at him. "...and we got mouse problems. There's a cat there, but one isn't enough."

"Ohhh" Thomas said knowingly, nodding his head. He headed toward my corner and pointed at the fat, healthy looking cat across from my cage. "This one looks like it was born to catch mice." He told the man.

The sailor cast one look at the cat. "Too fat!" He grumbled then started looking around until he spotted me.

"And what do we have here?" He said coming to me. "This one looks scrappy. What's his story?" Thomas hurried over to his side.

"This one was caught few days ago. He's a stray." Thomas told him.

The sailor's eyes gleamed. "He healthy?" he asked.

"Oh, yes. Very!" the boy answered. "He's a bit thin, but that'll just make him a better hunter."

"I'll take him." he said decisively, backing away with his arms folded, looking at me measuringly.

Thomas nodded and carefully opened the door of my cage. I tried to flee, but

Thomas grabbed me by the scruff and pulled me out. I squirmed to get free, growling and hissing, but it was no use.

The sailor's eyes were watching me closely. He had piercing blue eyes which made me shiver. "Small, but strong." the man said, sounding satisfied. "He'll do."

Thomas pushed me into a small cardboard cage with holes in the side of it. I had to push my face up against the side and look out one of the holes with one eye.

I remembered Skipper and Greif raced through my belly at the thought of him. But my sadness quickly turned into fear as man jerked my cage up. It swayed back and forth sickeningly, and I unsheathed my claws to grip the ground, but even so, I slid back and forth inside the cage as he walked.

We exited the cage room, and entered the main office. Thomas went to the counter and grabbed piece of paper as the man clunked me down roughly on the countertop. "Your name, sir?" he asked, grabbing a pen.

"Diego Carter." The man grumbled. Thomas wrote that, and a few other things on the paper.

"He's yours now." Thomas said placing one copy of the paper in the drawer and handing another copy to Diego. "Have a nice day."

Diego grunted a dismissive reply, and promptly carried me out of the pound. I was sure glad to get out of that place, however, I was still afraid of what would happen to me next.

Diego opened the back door of a black car and put my cage there. Then, he opened the front, and got in himself. There was a roaring of an engine that vibrated through my cage as the car started and we drove away.

I remembered the last time I'd been in a car, with Terrah. Memories flooded back, making me sigh, and I rested my chin on my paws, closing my eyes in grief as a tear rolled down my cheek.

****

Hours passed. It had been a bumpy ride, and many times I felt like throwing up.

Finally, we stopped. I breathed deeply in relief, but I could only see out through some small air holes in my cage. Diego got out, and roughly snatched me out, which made me feel even sicker.

As I peered out to see the surroundings, I gaped. There was endless blue water just in front of us. *'This must be the ocean.'* I thought.

It was indigo blue, and the sunlight made it shimmer. The glare made my eyes squint, but I couldn't take them off the view.

A few minutes later, we approached a very big ship. I gulped as Diego started going up the long walkway, swinging me along, dangling me over the water as he climbed up toward the ship's railing.

"G-Afternoon, Garry." Diego murmured to a man reading a newspaper. Garry stood up.

"Afternoon, sir" Garry said. "'We're finished loading, and ready to shove off."

Diego nodded briskly, walking past him.

We got to the top floor where Diego released me. Surprised and pleased, I bolted out, checking if there was a bigger cage or not. There wasn't, and I was free for the first time in a while. It felt good, and I ran forward fast, trying to get as far away from Diego as possible in case he changed his mind about letting me go.

I was looking back while I was running, checking if anyone was following. But just then, I spotted a gray blur right in front of me, and I skittered into a stop, afraid I would crash. I found myself nose to nose with a gray tabby cat. It was a girl, and she stared at me, her eyes narrow. She had a nick in both ears, so I figured she had been in some tough fights. But she looked healthy and well fed. She stared at me blankly, her expression impossible to read.

I stepped back, uncomfortable. I'd never been around girl cats before, other than my mother and my sisters. "Uh... I'm sorry if I bothered you." I stammered. "I'll just be on my way now."

"To where?" the she-cat had a hard edgy voice. I suddenly realized I didn't know where I should go now.

"Um...off of this ship, I guess?" I answered.

"No!" She hissed. "There's no way out of here." Her emerald eyes blazed like green fire.

My heart sank. She sounded a bit crazy. "Are you sure?" I asked.

"Of course! I've lived here nearly as long as I can remember." she growled.

I sighed heavily. The she-cat eyed me up and down. "You must be the new cat here." She observed. "I'm Shira."

I fumbled for words. Terrah didn't give me any name, and neither did Skipper.

"I'm not sure I have a name. But I think my owner used to call me Kitty." I told her. I felt a little embarrassed, not having a name.

Shira snorted. "Kitty?" she asked mockingly. "That's cute." she added scornfully. "It's a bad sign. Humans who don't name their pets don't care about you that much."

I bristled. When I first saw Shira, I didn't think she looked like a nice cat, but now, I was sure. "How do you know? I'm pretty sure *you* didn't have an owner." I retorted. "But you have a name. How do you explain that?"

"I named myself." She explained curtly. "I had an owner once when I was a kitten…" She paused pain clouding her eyes. Then she changed the subject.

"Okay, *Kitty.* Do you know how to catch mice?" She said my name with a disdainful tone, which I tried my best to ignore.

"I fought a rat before." I said, trying to sound authoritative.

"Do - you - know - how - to - catch - mice?" she repeated slowly, as though I were stupid and couldn't understand the question. I ignored that too. "Technically, no." I answered.

"Urrghh." Shira growled, shaking her head. "The sailors bought you to catch mice. So you have to catch mice!" she hissed with irritation.

"What happens if I don't?" I asked.

"Nothing really. You starve and die." She shrugged when she said it, like it was no big deal.

I gulped. "Starve? Don't they feed us?"

"Who? Sailors?" she snorted. "Of course they don't feed us."

"Why?"

Shira rolled her eyes. "Because they think if we're not hungry, we won't catch mice. It's a good thing you know how to fight rats. There's an awful lots of rats around here."

"Oh." I said, feeling very ignorant and immature.

"Well, good luck." Shira said before turning away.

I sat there for a moment, watching her walk away and feeling self conscious, thinking that was a very uncomfortable conversation.

Suddenly there was a blast of an amazingly loud horn, and I almost jumped out of my skin. Then I felt a strange vibration in the metal floor of the ship, and a bunch of seagulls flew off the railing far in front of me. I crouched down for a moment, not knowing what was happening. But then it seemed like the whole world started to move. I ran over to the side of the ship and looked out over the edge.

We were moving, slowly at first, but it was making me really nervous. I stood there and watched for a long time, and we kept getting farther and farther away from land.

As I stood there, it started to become very clear that there would be no chance of getting away now. I contemplated that for a while, and finally, I turned back, looking around with a greater interest in my new home.

There were walkways with open doors all over the place, and it seemed like I could go anywhere I wanted to go. Nobody seemed to care, or even to notice me.

I stepped gingerly through one of the doorways, and into a long hallway that smelled like oil. Everything smelled like oil, and I wrinkled my nose in distaste.

I started exploring the ship, and soon I was feeling better. It was really a huge place, and I had all the freedom I wanted. But I had a lot of questions to, so I started looking for Shira.

There were not many humans on the ship. I think there were only about 20 sailors, and most of them didn't even look at me when I passed them. They just did their work and mostly ignored me. One guy was especially mean though, and always tried to kick at me, or throw something at me whenever he saw me. But he smelled like pipe smoke and I could smell him from a mile away so I just avoided him.

After a number of hours wandering around, I was starting to get hungry. It was getting dark, and the sky was cloudy and grey. I hadn't seen Shira, and I hadn't seen any mice. Actually, I still didn't like the idea of eating mice, but I had eaten a couple of them since I had been abandoned by my family, so I resigned myself.

But right now, I just wanted some food. I remembered the days when Skipper and I had stolen food from Humans to survive, and in my wanderings I had discovered the ship's Kitchen, and the place where the sailors gathered to eat. I decided to head that way and see if I could steal a little food.

The eating place was loud and busy. They were having supper and the smell of it, made my mouth water.

My eyes suddenly caught sight of a chunk of meat that one of the sailors dropped. I smiled and slowly approached the meat, keeping my body low against the floor. I grabbed it and was trying to run away, when the sailor who dropped it spotted me.

"You dirty little rat." He cursed. A couple of bad words I shouldn't mention came along. He kicked me hard, and I flew through the air, losing my grip on the meat. The sailors laughed. "We'll have to watch that one. He's a thief." I heard the sailor say as I flitted away.

Embarrassed and hungry, I started hunting for mice. *'Maybe all the mice are hiding down deep inside the ship.'* I thought, heading away from the galley, working my way along corridors and down many stairs.

'Mice come out at night.' I told myself, *'...and they like dark places where they can find crumbs.'* I tried to think like a mouse, but it wasn't easy. The

hallways below deck had dim lights, but most of the rooms were entirely dark, and I entered one that smelled like there might be some mice around.

I went into my hunting crouch, and slithered across the floor. Suddenly, I could see two green eyes glowing menacingly at me in the dark. I stiffened my hackles, thinking that must be the biggest mouse in the world. But then I relaxed as the emerald eyes moved forward, revealing the face that they belonged to. "Shira!" I cried, feeling relieved. "You scared me out of my fur! I'm trying to catch some mice."

Shira snorted. "I was watching you." She said mockingly. "Do you call that a hunting crouch? It looked like you had to go to the bathroom."

I bristled, but I had learned to laugh at myself, so I tried not to take offense. "Oh, really? Let's see if you do better then." I growled.

"Well, you scared them all away." She turned away, and walked out the door. "Follow me if you want, but be quiet." she said coldly, as though she didn't care if I did or not.

She moved slowly, sniffing the air as she creped along. I could see her choosing which way to go by the tiny smells in the air. I closed my eyes, trying to smell what she smelled, and there, faintly, I could detect the faint scent of mice.

Shira silently went into a crouch, and I examined how her legs were positioned under her. Her back claws were extended, getting the best grip possible on the metal floor. There was a slight movement ahead, behind some boxes that were stacked against the wall.

With her tail barely touching the ground, she slipped forward as silently as snake. I watched her, impressed, trying to remember exactly what she did so that I could do it the same way later.

Shira dropped all the way down, stopping for a careful moment about a meter away from the mouse, and then she pounced squarely on its back. Before it could even squeak in surprise, she gave it a quick bite at the spine, and the mouse went limp in her jaws.

She gave me a challenging and smug look. "Now your turn." She said. With the mouse in her mouth, it sounded more like; "mow yurpum"

I nodded, and then took a deep breath, partly to calm myself, and partly to check the smell of mice. I began to work my way out of the room we were in, down the hallway in search of new prey.

At first I couldn't smell any mice, except for the one Shira caught. She was carrying it along as she followed me down the hallways. I concentrated harder, and closed my eyes. Then, I opened them just a slit as I got a whiff of a mouse.

I followed the scent trail, dropping low. I remembered to keep my tail low, and slowly, cautiously moved forward.

Behind a clump of boxes in another dark room, a mouse was sniffing around looking for crumbs. My heart beat in suspense and I dropped into a crouch, keeping my paws under my belly so I could put more energy into the jump.

I pounced and landed with my front paws slamming at the mouse. I unsheathed my claws so it couldn't escape. The mouse squealed in terror, and my face wrinkled excitedly at the sound. I quickly gave it a bite, and the squeal stopped.

Happily, with the mouse hanging limp in my jaws, I padded over to Shira, tail high. Shira looked a bit impressed, but I wouldn't know it by what she said. "Not bad for the first time. But you should've killed it before it squealed. Now all the mice around here must've ran away."

I shrugged, setting the mouse down in front of me. "I don't care." I told her. "One is all I need right now." I glanced at the mouse and licked my lips. I was hungry, and the smell of it made my mouth water.

I practiced my skill more that night by myself. I didn't really like Shira watching me, and she seemed to like being alone. I caught 3 more mice, and made sure to bite them before they could squeal. I saved the last one, and went to find Shira, offering to share it with her, but she refused, turning away coldly. She might have been jealous about how fast I learned, but I think she had been alone on that ship so long that she just didn't know how to have friends. I decided to try hard to gain her trust and friendship.

Early in the morning, while it was still dark, I felt pretty exhausted, because hunting is tiring work. It takes a lot of concentration. My stomach was round for the first time in a long while, and that made me even more sleepy.

I made my way up to the top deck where the air was fresh and cool, and spent a little while just sitting by the railing, looking at the huge sea. I never imagined there was so much water in the whole world, and I really didn't like water. But I felt safe and peaceful there on the ship. I was feeling pretty satisfied with life, when I heard the sound of footsteps behind me.

I turned my head, trying to act like a cat who doesn't care much, but inside, I worried that it might be the mean sailor who had kicked me earlier last night. Fortunately, it wasn't. It was a skinny blond haired boy with a lot of freckles on his face. In one hand, he held a broom, and a bucket of water was in the other hand. He saw me and cautiously stepped forward. I flattened my ears and studied his every move.

When he took one step forward, I took a step back.

"Here, kitty, kitty, kitty" The boy called. I was surprised. Only Terrah had called me Kitty. I felt a stab of pain in the memory, but I warmed up a little bit to this kid. He took a step forward again, and this time, I stayed where I was. After a while, he and I were only a meter away from each other.

Suddenly He turned around and dashed away saying, "Wait here." So I waited, and after a few moments he came back with a carton that looked so familiar. Milk! I realized. I licked my lips. Terrah used to give me milk all the time. He poured it into a bowl and I padded over to him, meowing.

I lapped energetically at the milk and purred contentedly at the rich taste. The boy reached out his hand to pet me and I stiffened for a moment, then relaxed, focusing on the sweet milk while he stroked my fur.

It felt just like how Terrah used to pet me when I ate, only this guy didn't smell like apples. He smelled like a mix of cheese and dirty socks. I purred louder anyway, and swished my long tail happily around his ankles. He laughed with joy, and started talking to me. "Hey, little guy, I'm Pete. What's your name?"

I meowed back. "I'm not sure." I told him. "But Terrah used to call me Kitty."

"What was that? Your name is Kitty?" he answered, seeming to understand.

"Yes!" I meowed, quite surprised that he'd called me by the right name.

'Okay, I'll come back later, but now I need to clean up the deck." he said, standing up and backing away.

"Okay." I meowed.

Pete smiled and went away, and I went back to the milk. I was still greedily lapping at it when a snarl sounded in my ear. "I saw you." came Shira's voice.

"So what?" I grumbled in a distracted way, not looking up.

"I saw your rubbing on that human." She growled. "That was a disgusting scene for me to watch."

"I don't get it." I replied, looking up from my milk. "The boy was nice." I snapped at her a little defensively. "And he gave me milk."

Shira looked at me as though I were stupid. "You can't trust humans. How do you know there isn't poison in that milk." she queried, hissing through her teeth disapprovingly, and narrowing her eyes at me.

"There isn't!" I hissed back at her. "I'm ok right now, aren't I?" I took a deep breath and calmed down, thinking maybe I was misunderstanding her. She had obviously had some kind of bad experiences with humans. "Why don't you try some. It's really tasty." I told her, forcing a friendly voice and deciding to try kindness.

"I'm a cat, not a human!" she screeched shrilly, suddenly swiping her paw at my face with her claws extended.

I yowled in pain as her claws raked across my forehead. I totally was not expecting that, and jumped back, uncertain of how to respond. "I was just trying to be nice!" I howled, but anger was welling up in my chest. "But I'm not now." I hissed, and jumped up on her, my claws flashing as I hooked her on her shoulder, feeling her skin tear a little under my blow.

She growled, and flipped her body sideways in a move that took me completely by surprise. Before I knew what happened, I was pinned under her, my forelegs trapped under her paws.

Wildly, I tried to kick her off with my hind legs, but she was too strong, and she reached down, closing her sharp teeth over my throat. In that moment, I thought I was going to die. I stopped wriggling and braced myself, my life flashing before my eyes. But the fatal bite never came.

My eyes were still closed when I felt her weight lifting from me, and I rolled over to see her sitting calmly on the deck, licking her shoulder which was bleeding slightly.

"I didn't like you the first time I set my eyes on you." She said. "But now I hate you. Stay away from me. I'll kill you next time if you don't." She spoke calmly, and then walked away.

I stared after her, dumfounded, wondering what just happened.

Chapter 7

Many months past, or maybe a year. I tried to avoid Shira most of the time because I knew what she could do and I didn't want to get killed.

I understood her though. It was like me thinking all the dogs were bad, only with her it was humans. But I didn't have the nerve to say what I thought to her, and it probably wouldn't have helped anyway.

After work, Pete would often steal some food from the kitchen to feed me. We became buddies, and I sometimes spent some time in his cabin with him.

Occasionally, the ship would go to land, and I knew it before we actually docked because of the smell. Land has many more smells than the ocean has. But most of the time the ship would stay at sea, and smaller boats would carry stuff back and forth, to and from land.

There were many storms, and they were terrifying because the ship would rock, and the wind would howl. I couldn't go outside during a storm because if I did, I'd get blown away or be swallowed up by one of the big waves that would wash entirely over the ship. But staying inside was dangerous too, because sometimes things would fall when the ship started rolling and rocking on the massive waves. I usually hid under something on one of the lower decks until the storm stopped. But those were small storms compared to the one that changed the lives of Shira and me.

That day the sky turned dark almost like night, even though it was still the middle of the day. The wind and waves came first, and soon water was washing over the upper decks. All the sailors hurried to secure things so that they could go inside. Then they came in and closed all the doors tight. I watched them try to make the ship safe from anything that could move around, and finally, I headed for the lower decks as the storm got worse and the ship started rolling and rocking sickeningly.

I had been through enough storms by now, but it was still hard to control my fear. '*It will be ok.*' I told myself, breathing deeply and trying to relax.

The room I was hiding in was full of boxes that were stacked on shelves, and all the shelves had short fronts on them that held everything in place. But the ship was rocking so badly, that it looked like the boxes were about to fall. The room's heavy steel door was swinging back and forth, creaking and groaning like a sick old man.

I stiffened at the sound of a loud crash, and I turned to see Shira jumping off a shelf as some boxes finally came crashing down. She had been hiding in there, but I didn't realize it because I had been so distracted by the storm.

Suddenly there was another loud bang, and it felt like the boat was flipping all the way over on its side. The door slammed into the wall with frightening force, and the sound was deafening. At the same time, more boxes started falling down, one of them landing right in front of me. That was more than I could stand, and I jumped out of my hiding place as even more boxes fell, crashing all around me.

Shira was surprised and frightened too. She kept peering around nervously, not able to decide where to go since boxes were falling around us on every side now. But we couldn't stay there.

"Run!" I yelled, and dashed toward the open doorway, sliding and staggering drunkenly as the floor moved beneath my paws. Shira didn't reply, but I could hear her running behind me, and I could feel her whiskers on the tip of my tail. I ran as hard as I could, but the door was swinging toward us fast.

Closing my eyes, I put out an extra burst of energy, and launched forward as if I was hunting a mouse.

I felt the wind from the door, and heard Shira's yowl of pain all at the same time. I came skidding to a stop, and turned around, to see what had happened. Shira's leg was stuck in the door. It was crushed and bleeding. I ran to help her. I grabbed her by the scruff and started pulling, but the door was wedged shut, trapping her leg, and it wouldn't budge. Shira hissed in pain.

I bit my lips, anxious of what I could do to help her. Then, my eyes caught the door handle. '*Of course!*' I thought. '*I can open this door the way Skipper taught me!'*

"I'll get you out of there, Shira." I told her. Gathering my haunches, I leaped into the air, and grabbed the handle the way I'd succeeded with Skipper. The door clinked and opened a little bit.

Shira stumbled out gasping. Her leg was squished, and it was twisted and crushed into a weird angle. I nosed her gently. "Are you okay?" I asked.

"Yeah, I guess." She mumbled though gritted teeth. I could see that she was lying, and that she was trying not to show her pain. I glanced at her leg. It was bloody, and even more blood was oozing out. It looked really bad.

"Wait here. I'll get help." I told her, trying to catch her eye.

Shira groaned, but didn't say anything. With one last look, I dashed out as fast as I could toward Pete's room. Luckily, Pete was inside because of the storm.

I wailed loudly. Pete looked up. "You're okay! I was worried about you!" he exclaimed. "Are you hungry?"

I wailed again and went out the door, pausing to see if Pete was following. "It's Shira! She's hurt!" I mewed urgently. Pete didn't seem to understand, but followed me anyway, curious. I guess he could tell that I was upset and something was wrong.

I lead him downstairs in rapid steps. I spotted Shira crouching in the hallway, and bounded over to see if she was all right. "Shira!" I said. "I brought help."

She lifted her head dully. Her eyes shone with fear and panic when she saw Pete. She wriggled desperately to get away from him, but her leg wouldn't move, and she fell limp gasping.

"He's okay." I told Shira. "He's going to help you."

Pete looked at Shira surprised. "What happened?" He asked bewildered. "Wait, I'll get some medical stuff."

As Pete dashed away, Shira glared at me angrily. "What - Did - You - Do!" She managed to snarl.

"I brought help!" I told her defensively, but with confidence in my voice.

"No! You brought a *human!*" She growled.

"You don't understand!" I mewed. "You think there're only bad humans out there. But you're *wrong*. There are as many good humans as there are bad ones."

Shira snorted weakly. Just then, Pete came running toward us with a first aid kit and some food. He gently lifted Shira up, but she thrust her forepaws out, resisting and hissing weakly.

"It's okay." Pete soothed her. "I'm just wrapping this cloth around your leg so it'll stop the bleeding. I'm sorry. I'm not

a doctor, so that's all I can do for you."
Pete sighed.

When Shira's leg was all wrapped like a cocoon, Pete poured milk into a bowl, and opened a tuna can. The sound of the can opening and the smell of tuna made my mouth water, but I stayed silent because the food was for Shira.

A man's husky voice echoed through the hall way. "Pete? You down there? Come here and mop this mess on the top deck."

"Coming!" Pete yelled. He turned to us. "Eat a little okay? Some water got in the ship, and I gotta go." He said, then hurried up the stairs.

I nudged Shira with my nose. "Come on." I told her. "Eat." With my paw, I slid the tuna closer to her.

Shira glanced at it uncertainly and hesitated. "I... No, I can't." She said.

"Why not?"

"It's human food!" Shira growled.

"If you don't eat it, you might starve." I reasoned.

"I'll hunt." she argued.

"With that leg?" I countered. She glared at me, and her nostrils flared. "Come on." I said. "Just this once."

Shira glanced at the tuna, then back at me again, faltering. The smell of it must have been driving her crazy. "Fine!" she resolved.

Pete's bandage stayed on for a long time, and Shira couldn't use her bad leg at all. She developed this hopping limp, and she hated it when people watched her trying to get around. She couldn't hunt, of course, so I had to hunt for her. She really hated that too, and the first time I brought her a mouse was really hard for both of us.

Shira also had to get used to human food. For a while, Pete would bring food to her, but before long, she would sometimes follow me to his room for a snack. But she would never let him touch her. Over the weeks, however, little by little, she slowly started to change.

One day, after her bandage fell off, Shira was sitting beside a railing, her paws tucked under her, and her tail wrapped around them. I padded over to her with a plump mouse dangling from my jaws and plopped it down in front of her. "Here." I said, and turned away to look out over the water. I knew she didn't like me to watch her when I brought her a mouse. But then, she did something that really surprised me.

"Hey Kitty." She said. "Do you want to share this?"

I turned around and looked at her. I was so shocked, I didn't know what to say. But I knew I shouldn't show it or she would get mad. "Sure." I purred, like it was her normal behavior.

We tugged the mouse, sharing pieces together, and didn't talk. When we finished, Shira paused, licking her paw, seemingly embarrassed. Then she said, "I just want to say I'm sorry I fought you before and said that I hated you." She paused for a moment and then continued. "I guess you were right about humans too. Maybe not all of them are bad."

I blinked. "I understand. I felt the same way about dogs until I met a good one." I said. Thinking of Skipper made my eyes warm.

Shira looked at me skeptically. "Dogs? That's just hard to believe." She said, but she was purring.

I purred too. "Believe it or not, it's true. I'll tell you about Skipper some day."

We remained silent after that until Shira spoke again. "I used to be a pet." she confessed.

"Oh, yeah?" I said surprised.

Shira nodded. "My owner was bad. He drank something from a bottle every day, and he hit and kicked me all the time." She rolled over on her side to show a long jagged scar and a patch of skin where her fur wouldn't grow.

I winced. "Ouch." I said sympathetically.

"I got that scar when I was a few months old. I ran away then, when I was just a kitten, but I got caught by an animal shelter. They fixed my side, but they almost killed me in the end. The sailors took me then. It saved my life, but they never cared about me." Shira explained.

She looked like she needed a hug. But I wouldn't dare try it. She continued. "I never told that to anyone before."

"I'm glad you told me." I mewed, and pressed to her side trying to comfort her. I didn't want to say too much. I didn't know how she would respond, so I just tried to be a good listener.

"Well," Shira said. She sniffed and stood up. "You go rest now. You had a big hunt." Then, she padded away awkwardly on her three good legs. I realized right then, that her crooked leg would never heal. I sat and sadly watched her limp away.

Chapter 8

A few months went by, and Shira and I were closer than ever. We ate together, played together, and slept together. We were like two peas in a pod.

Shira was getting quite plump, since Pete had been feeding her and me every night. At least I thought that was why, until she gave me some very shocking news.

That day, we were waiting for Pete to come with fresh milk and tuna. I noticed that Shira was acting weird. She jumped every time I said something, and sat as far away from me as possible.

I narrowed my eyes thoughtfully and decided to ask her why. I tiptoed over to her. "What's wrong?" I asked gently.

Shira stiffened. "What? No. Nothing's wrong." She blabbered. She seemed nervous, but I had never seen her nervous before, so I wasn't sure.

I blinked. "Nothing's wrong? Are you sure?" I prompted.

Shira nodded feebly. There was a long silence. She kept looking at her paws. Finally, she spoke. "Okay! I'll tell you."

I pricked my ears.

Shira took a deep breath. She exhaled, then inhaled again. She continued doing that, and I waited with patience, watching her curiously. Finally she opened her mouth and spoke fast. "I'm pregnant." she blurted.

I gaped. I just stood there with my mouth opened for a whole minute. It was so surprising and shocking. Shira shifted her weight on her paws, embarrassed.

"Am... am I the father?" I asked.

Shira rolled her eyes. "Do you see any other boy cats around here?" She mewed with irritation. "I knew you'd hate it. I'm sorry. I hate it as much as you do."

"Hate it?" I exclaimed. "I *love* it!" I bounded over to her excitedly and brushed against her pelt, purring like an engine.

Shira blinked, looking surprised and relieved. "Really?"

"Yes!" I purred happily. "I'm going to be a father!"

Shira purred. I nosed her round belly. "I'm your father." I whispered. Shira laughed. "You're not exactly modest."

she said and I purred even more deeply.

Pete never came, but we didn't mind, and we sat there together, watching the twinkling stars side by side.

****

Over the next few days, we talked about our family, and thought it wouldn't be good to have kittens on this ship. The people were often mean, and we didn't know what they might do to our kits. Besides, there were a lot of dangers on board, and we didn't have any help from anyone except Pete. He was okay, but not the most responsible guy in the world.

We decided to wait until the next time we smelled land, when we knew the ship would go to the dock. Then we would make our escape.

The time came on a cold day sometime during the winter. I didn't worry too much because I knew how to get food a bunch of different ways, and I had lived most of my life off the ship already. But it was difficult for Shira. She was resolved though, so we planned our escape.

They always sent a bunch of boxes to land whenever we docked, and then they brought a lot of new ones on again. We were pretty good at getting in boxes, and we had already found some that were full of blankets. It was good, because Shira was getting pretty heavy, and she would be warm and comfortable in a blanket box.

It was still dark in the morning, and the sun was just glowing on the horizon when we snuck into the box. I hooked the lid with one of my claws and pulled it down so that no one would notice us, and we settled down to wait. It took a while, but finally, we felt the pile of boxes start to move, and we held on nervously as we were lifted into the air.

There were loud engine noises from some monstrous machines, and the smell of smoke nearly choked us. After a while, we could hear a man's voice yelling, "These boxes go in the New York truck!" Another voice answered faintly. We felt our boxes move off in another direction, finally thumping down, surprising us and making us jump.

"New York." I thought to myself. The name of that place brought back memories of my last days with Terrah, and I felt a pang in my heart. I thought I had gotten over her many times, but by now, I knew that part of me never would. The thought that I might be moving closer to her made my heart beat faster and filled me with conflicted emotion. But I kept that to myself because I knew Shira wouldn't understand.

There was a grunt as a man with strong body odor carried us. He threw our box onto the metal floor of a big truck, and we scrambled out as the door closed with a slam. Everything was dark. We were in a truck full of boxes similar to the one we hid in.

The truck rumbled as the engine started, and soon after, we felt the it start moving. Shira and I were silent as we examined the inside of the truck, but there wasn't really much to explore.

Later we got hungry. I had done some extra hunting just to get ready for the trip, and we pulled a mouse out of the box to share.

I don't know how many days we were in the truck. The sun would shine through cracks in the door, but we didn't count the days. There were a couple of times that Shira heaved a big sigh and leaned into me as uncertainty about our future flooded over her. We were both afraid, but I tried not to show it for her sake.

From time to time the truck stopped for a while, and then started moving again. We guessed the driver had to sleep, but he never opened the door. There was always the strong smell of gas and exhaust smoke, and it made Shira sick. I got used to it pretty quick, but it really bothered her.

Finally, on a very cold day, the door was opened, and we quickly hid in our box. Before long, we were carried again and set down in a building. As soon as we were sure that nobody was around, I pushed the lid up and peered out to see if it was safe.

"Okay." I told Shira. "We can go out now."

Shira limped out, setting her paws onto the ground. Her eyes became round with wonder and interest. She seemed surprised at how still the ground was, and both of us stumbled forward. We were not used to being on land, and riding for days in the truck hadn't helped us. I purred, amused, and Shira just smiled at me, laughter shining in her eyes as we staggered around together until we adjusted.

The place was pretty big, and it was full of tall racks that had many boxes stacked on them. It was late, so there were no people there and we had the entire building to ourselves. I lifted my nose and took in the odors, trying to detect food.

We had saved five mice, and brought them with us in the box, but I had been missing fish and milk. Mouse was ok when it was fresh, but after a few days, it was not really pleasant to eat. We had one left, but neither of us really wanted to eat it.

I could smell fresh mouse in the warehouse, and that was good, but I could also smell human food somewhere toward the back of the building. It was cold in the warehouse, much colder than it was on the ship, and Shira was shivering. She tried to hide it, but I could feel it because we were sitting close together.

"Let's go back there." I told her, starting toward the back part of the building. Shira nodded. She could smell the food too, and we both knew that where humans stayed, it was usually warmer. We walked together, keeping off to the side along the walls or behind the boxes, trying to stay hidden as much as possible.

There was a long wall of offices with a hallway that went between them, and it had carpet on the floor. The smell was coming from ahead, and it led us to a closed door where we stopped.

"It's here." Shira said, her nostrils flaring out as she sniffed the air. "Can you open it like you did before?" she asked, looking up at the handle.

I nodded and jumped lightly upwards. I had been doing this for years, and had developed a real knack for it. In just a moment, the door swung open, and we could see into the room. Faint moonlight shone through some windows and showed us the way.

"It is like the galley on the ship." Shira said, walking in ahead of me. "I can smell the food."

It was warmer in the cafeteria than it was out in the hallway. "Yeah. We can get out of the cold and maybe find something to eat." I said.

Shira snorted. Then she yawned as though I had reminded her how cold and tired she was.

"Come on." I meowed. "Let's find a place to sleep."

Shira didn't object. "That's a good idea." She said in a drowsy voice.

In the back of the room, there was a bunch of chairs stacked up against the wall, and behind those chairs was a heater. It wasn't very warm, but it felt like a dream to us. It was wonderful, and the area was hidden, so we felt somewhat secure. We both lay down, and I must have fallen asleep as soon as my head hit my paws.

Chapter 9

I woke up and blinked sleep out of my eyes, glancing around, forgetting for a moment where I was. But then I remembered where we were, and our entire adventure came flooding back into my mind.

I looked at the place Shira had been sleeping, but she wasn't there. Panic and fear touched my mind as I imagined what might have happened to her and my kittens.

"Shira?" I called nervously, not wanting to make too much noise.

"What?" Shira spoke from behind me. She had something in her mouth.

"Shira!" I exclaimed rushing toward her. "Where on Earth have you been? I was worried something had happened to you."

"I found food." Shira growled in an irritated tone. "I've survived my entire life without you, and I'm capable on my own" She retorted. "I don't need a babysitter."

"It's not that." I soothed her. "It's just that we're family now, and we have to look out for each other."

Her expression softened. "Ok. That's not so bad." She meowed. "I guess I'm not used to thinking like that. Come on, let's eat."

Our last mouse was smelling pretty bad, and there was no way either of us would even touch it. But we hadn't eaten for more than a day and were really hungry. "What do you have there?" I asked her, licking my lips in anticipation.

"Half a hamburger, I think. There was some bread, but I just brought the meat." She pushed it toward me, sliding it across the floor.

"What about you?" I asked. "You should eat first. You have kittens to feed."

"I already ate something." She said, narrowing her eyes at me.

I figured that maybe I should stop worrying about her so much before she got really mad, so I just took a big bite of the hamburger, closed my eyes, and enjoyed it. It was a bit cold, but it was fresh and delicious, except for the little catsup that was still on it. I don't like catsup.

"Why didn't you eat it all?" Shira asked me when I had finished eating. "I'm full." I lied. "We can save it, or you can eat it. You have kittens to feed, and I don't."

Shira sighed. "Fine." She said, and took a bite out of the hamburger meat.

While she ate, we discussed a little about what we should do. I wanted to stay there, hunting mice in the warehouse and stealing human food from the cafeteria at night, but Shira said that this place was too dangerous for her kittens. Even after the time with Pete, she was still distrustful of humans. So finally, we decided that we would move out of there right away and try to find somewhere that was suitable to raise a family.

After she was done, we headed out. It was still early and the warehouse was locked, but we found an air vent in the side of the building and were able to scrunch our bodies through it and get outside.

Shira had not been on land for so long that it all seemed new to her. Her eyes were big, and for a while she had a hard time walking because she was not watching where she was going.

Before long though, she grew more accustom to the strange, huge, and wonderfully unpredictable world, and we were able to progress along more quickly on our mission.

The area around the warehouse was mostly parking lots and huge metal buildings. It didn't look too promising for us, because there was no easy source of food. We needed to find a place where there were people, but also a place that we felt safe. As I thought about it, I felt uncertain that we would ever find somewhere like that.

We walked until we reached a busy street. All the other streets we'd seen until now had been almost deserted, but this one was not.

We stood there frozen, watching the cars flash by, and Shira gasped, stepping back nervously as the cars whizzed past. "How are we going to get to the other side?" She mewed dreadfully.

"I have no idea." I said, feeling a bit upset to my stomach. We couldn't give up now, but there was a chance that we might have our bones chopped by those cars. And with Shira's bad leg, the chance of that happening was big.

"Maybe we can run when there's a big gap between the cars." Shira suggested hopefully.

I scowled at her skeptically. "I doubt it." I said. "Even if there was a big gap, you wouldn't manage with that leg." I angled my ears toward Shira's back leg.

She looked angrily at me sideways for a moment, and then sighed, knowing that I was right. "Then what should we do?" She mewed.

I looked around dismayed. *'If only we could fly…'* I thought to myself looking up. I narrowed my eyes, expecting the sun to shine in my face, but something up there was blocking it. It was a bridge that I hadn't noticed before, and it was leading to the other side!

"We need to get up there." I said pointing my tail to the bridge.

Hope flashed in Shira's eyes. "Of course!" She exclaimed. "Why didn't we see it before?"

We headed to the bridge rapidly, going up a steep dirt hill and into the grass beside the roadway that went over to the other side. But it was not as simple as it had looked from down below. There were a lot of people walking across, and it seemed like a dangerous thing to try walking together with them.

I was still sitting there watching the people and didn't notice at first that Shira had found a narrow beam under the bridge. She had already started going across it. "Come on." she called over her shoulder. I hesitated, thinking that it looked dangerous too. We were pretty high up, and the beam was really narrow. The cars were zooming past below us, and if we fell down… I didn't want to think about it.

But all the time I was thinking, Shira just kept limping along, and she was almost half way across already. I gulped and followed her, having little choice now.

The sound of the cars frightened me, and I didn't dare look down. I focused on Shira's tail, which was lashing to and fro to help her keep balance. Before I knew it we were both across, but my heart was still pounding when Shira said. "Do you smell that?"

I had been too distracted to sniff the air, but her words made me take a big experimental breath. "Food." I said simply. From the smell it seemed like there was a lot of food in this area of town. That was a good sign.

We decided to follow the smell and find a place to spend the night. We snuck forward, trying to stay hidden as much as possible, and after a couple of blocks, we saw the restaurant signs.

"These stores are where Humans go to eat." I told Shira.

"You mean they can eat whenever they want?" she asked, looking fascinated. "On the ship there was only the galley, and everyone ate at the same time every day."

I shrugged, feeling a bit sad, remembering the time long ago when I used to be able to eat whenever I wanted too. "Yeah. It's different here though. They eat any old time they want too." I replied, and started moving forward again.

"Don't they get fat?" Shira asked me, as she limped along behind me.

"I've seen some fat ones, but I never knew any." I told her. "Hey, look at this place." I said, peering into a dark driveway that went around behind a fish restaurant.

Shira followed my eye. "Oooh!" She said licking her lips. "Let's go back there."

It was quiet, and it was dark. Maybe it would turn out to be the kind of place where we could hide safely. "Ok. It's a good place to explore."

We found a trashcan with a bunch of food scraps in it. Shira chose a fish head that we shared. It was a good place to find food, but it was too wet and fishy to sleep. Besides, there was no good place to hide, so we went further along the alley. It curved around behind the building into a dead end behind more restaurants with more garbage cans. It was a perfect place to get food.

There toward the end of the alley, where it ran up to a wall that had no doors or windows in it, we found a big truck with only 3 tires. It had a big box on the back of it, and ivy was growing over it, which meant that no humans used it anymore. It had been sitting there for a long time.

"I think this is it." I said as Shira jumped up on the truck for a closer look.

But before she could even answer, I heard her screech in surprise as a white cat with gray splotches sprang up from inside the truck, ramming into Shira. The strange cat was able to knock her down and pin her under him.

"Hey!" I hissed leaping to Shira's side. But Shira had recovered and gotten her good leg under her. In the blink of an eye, she had turned the tables on her attacker, flinging her opponent off her and crouching in a defensive stance.

He paused in his attack now, shaking his fur and staring at us with narrow eyes. I had time to examine him for the first time, and he was an odd looking character.

I noticed that he had a lot of scratches on his skin, and his fur was dusty and dull. His ears seemed a little too big for his head, and his whiskers were jet black, which looked strange standing out sharply against his white fur. But he was well fed, although one of his fangs was missing, and he had a network of scars on his face that made it look like a roadmap. An especially nasty scar ran across his left eye.

He came out of his crouch and growled menacingly. "This is my place. You don't just come marching into someone else's territory." he exclaimed with some authority. "You'd better turn your tails around and get out of here quick if you know what's good for you."

I certainly didn't want a fight with this cat. Why fight if you can use words? Shira bristled beside me.

I cleared my throat. "I'm sorry to interrupt you." I said nicely. "But my mate here is expecting my kittens, and she needs to rest." Shira glared at me, and so did the strange cat. "So I was wondering if we could shelter here." I continued.

The cat stared at me for a while, and for a moment, I thought he would let us.

"What did I say before?" The cat growled. "This is *my* place. If you want it, you have to fight for it!"

I gulped and turned around to tell Shira that maybe we should look somewhere else to stay, but Shira leaped past me, barreling into the cat, who yelped and clawed Shira across the back. She grunted in pain, and the cat grabbed her with his back legs and twisted, so it was now Shira who was pinned down.

With a loud battle cry, I leaped to Shira's rescue. I grabbed the enemy with my jaws and pulled him off her. She scrambled up coughing. The cat twisted itself to get free, and jumped on top of my back, digging his claws in my pelt.

I hissed in pain, thrusting my paws wildly. My claws hooked on his ear and he let go of me, yowling as blood trickled down his cheek.

Shira jumped to my side, flashing her paw toward the cat. He dodged, but got himself another nick in the ear.

Growling, the loner cat ducked underneath Shira, knocking her paws out from under her, and she stumbled. Then he pounced again, and as Shira tried to roll out of the way, he slashed his razor claws across her exposed belly.

"No!!!" I roared, and I ran with all my force, knocking the cat off Shira. Surprise lit his gaze, and I didn't take my claws off him as we rolled.

He pushed with force, and so did I. We wrestled, growling and hissing. With panic, I realized that the cat was aiming for my throat. I had no choice but do the same, because if not, I might get killed.

I flashed my paw toward his throat, and I felt the touch of his neck skin and the pulse of his blood there. The time seemed to stop. He froze, looking at me, and I saw his fear. For a moment, I wondered whether I should kill him or not. Then I remembered what Shira did with me long ago when we fought on the ship. I released my grip on his throat and stepped back.

He stared at me, confused. I gazed at him with narrow eyes and my chin high. "Go!" I growled. "This is *my* place now. If you don't…" I unsheathed my claws.

The cat glared at me for a second, then turned, and limped away, mumbling curses.

After the cat was out of earshot, I hurried toward Shira's side. "Shira!" I called. "Are you okay?"

Shira whimpered. "Yeah." She groaned and struggled to stand up.

"Shh." I whispered. "Don't stand up." She sighed and fell limp on the cold ground.

I grabbed Shira by the scruff. The air was cold, and I didn't want her lying there freezing, so I helped her scramble inside the truck where it was warm and quite cozy. I laid Shira on the seat and curled beside her. We drifted into sleep.

Chapter 10

The air was especially cold when I woke up, and I was shivering. There was a strange filtered light coming in through the truck's windows, and I lifted my head curiously to see what was going on.

The first thing I noticed was that Shira was sitting out in the open. It had snowed the night before, and she was framed in the whiteness all around her. After enjoying the scene silently for a few moments, I remembered her injury from the day before. I had told her to stay inside, but obviously, she had ignored me and didn't listen.

Shira noticed that I was awake, and bounded clumsily over to me spraying snow all over the place.

"Isn't it crazy?" She exclaimed joyfully. "The snow's all tiny, but look what it has done!" She lashed her tail around in pleasure at the snow covered scene.

I purred in amusement. It had snowed when we were on the ship sometimes, but it always quickly melted away as soon as it reached the sea, or touched the ship. So it was the first time for Shira to actually play in it.

I sniffed her, anxious about the wound on her stomach. The bleeding had stopped in the night, and there was a good scab on it, but her frolicking had opened it a little. However, it wasn't so bad now and I figured it was nothing really serious

I didn't like snow. I hated the feeling of it mushing around my paws, and after a while, I knew I would be all wet and cold, especially my paws.

One good thing about snow however, was that you could see any tracks. Stepping cautiously where there was less snow, I took a quick trip around the truck to see if there had been any secret visitors while we slept. I was still a bit concerned about that angry white cat, but thankfully, the snow was undisturbed. It seemed as though this really was our new home.

I sat in a grassy spot under the truck to avoid snow, thinking about food. Just then, my eyes caught what seemed like foot prints, and I leaped toward them, forgetting my dislike of snow.

They were bird prints, and they seemed fresh. Even though there were garbage cans with food from the restaurants, I had developed a preference for fresh food, and I really enjoyed hunting. My eyes followed the trail and caught a sparrow, pecking something from the ground.

I smiled in satisfaction. Quickly but quietly, I crept toward it. But the snow made a crunching sound and the sparrow looked up in alarm.

I growled in frustration as the bird began to fly. However, I was really hungry, so I wouldn't give up.

I leaped into the air, reaching my arms up as high as I could. My claws hooked on the sparrow's feathers and it went crashing into the snow. Before it could recover and fly away again, I pounced and killed it quickly.

I carried it to Shira who had watched the whole show. "Nice catch." She mewed.

I grunted. "It was nothing." I said. Then, I noticed that her eyes were filled with sorrow. 'She must miss hunting, and what a good hunter she was.' I thought. I sighed. "Let's eat." I said awkwardly. I took a bite first, spitting out the feathers. The feathers don't taste good. They are just furry, and they dry out your mouth.

Shira did the same, and we ate, chatting with each other.

****

I jerked awake at the sound of Shira yowling. I immediately jumped to her side. She was all sweaty and was moaning in pain. "What's wrong?" I demanded.

Shira looked up and groaned. "The kittens…. coming…" She managed to say. Then she fell to the floor gasping.

"It's okay. It'll be over soon." I said licking her. I tried to act calm, but inside I was panicking hard.

Shira screeched and kicked me away. I could see that her teeth were clenched in pain. She looked at me dully. "Go….Wait outside!" She said gasping.

I looked at her uncertainly. "Are you sure?" I asked.

"GO!!!" Shira howled. I hurried outside.

I paced back and forth nervously. I could hear Shira growling and yowling in pain, and my paws itched to go in and help her. But I knew that I would be no help in there, so I waited outside for the yowling to ebb away.

Finally Shira's screeching died down and cautiously I peeked inside. She looked at me and smiled weakly. Her fur was all messy and wet with sweat, but by her belly lay six little kittens.

I gasped. "They're beautiful!" I exclaimed purring. "You did wonderfully."

Shira purred hoarsely. I sniffed the kittens, who were suckling fiercely. I noticed that one of them wasn't suckling, and pushed it gently with my nose toward Shira. The kitten didn't move.

I looked at Shira in alarm. "This one's not moving." I told her, quietly panicking inside. Shira immediately sniffed the kitten while I held my breath, praying it was not dead.

"It's too late." Shira spoke in a choking voice. I stood there breathing fast. "No…" I whispered, and my eyes watered.

Shira looked away. "Should we name the kittens?" She asked. I nodded silently as I moved the dead kitten out of sight.

There were five kittens to name. Two of them were gray, one dark, and one light. The light gray one was a copy of her mother. The other three were yellow like me. One was yellow all over, and one was yellow except his belly and his paws were white, like mine. The other one was mostly white, with a few yellow splashes.

We decided to name the dark gray kitten Hunter, and the silver one Echo.

The yellow one became Dagger. The yellow one with a white belly and paws was Nico. And the white kitten with yellow splashes, we named Amber.

"Good names." I purred, satisfied. Shira purred in agreement, grooming the kittens' fur.

Chapter 11

The kittens grew and grew. They opened their bright green and yellow eyes and mewled for milk. Their rat-like bodies became fluffy and soft, and their heads became twice as big. They had cute button noses.

Hunter was the most adventuresome, always wanting to go explore outside the truck, and eager to try new stuff. Dagger had the highest voice, and when he mewled for milk we had to flatten our ears to block the sound.

The days as a big family were great. Shira and I had wonderful times with the kittens. I remember the first time they went outside.

"Mommmmy!" Hunter squeaked. "Just *one* step out the truck? I *promise* we won't go anymore." The other kittens nodded vigorously.

"No." Shira told them. "You need a nap."

"But we're not sleepy, are we?" Nico mewed looking at his brothers and sisters for support.

"No we're not!" Amber squeaked.

I looked at Shira. "Maybe we should let them." I said. "Like they said; just a paw out the truck. It's not like they'll be catnapped as soon as they're outside." I pointed out.

Dagger bounced up and down eagerly. "Yes!" He squealed. "Daddy says it's okay!"

Shira glared at me, and I shrugged. "It's cold outside, and they need a *nap.*" she hissed at me.

"We're not tired!" Hunter yowled.

"Yes, mommy. Please let us be outside." Echo meowed, looking at Shira with pleading eyes.

"I'll be with them all the time." I promised.

Shira glared at me again. "Fine." She growled.

"Yes!!" Hunter mewled, butting Nico.

"Let's go!" Echo mewed, running as fast as her short legs would carry her.

"Oh, no you don't." I said, quickly grabbing her by the scruff before she could get out. "You said a *paw* out. And we go out *together.*"

Echo wriggled her legs. "Okay." She grumbled.

I took a step into the freezing weather first, and then allowed the kittens to do the same. I saw Shira watching anxiously from behind. Typically, adventuresome Hunter took the first step into the snow covered truck bed.

"What *is* this?" Hunter squeaked, sniffing the snow. "It's mushy! And *cold*!"

I purred in amusement, and the other kittens cautiously took a step into the snow.

"Brrrr! It's cold outside!" Dagger meowed.

"That's because it's winter" I told him. "When spring comes, it'll be warm, and in summer, it'll be hot."

"What's a winter, and what's a spring, and what's a summer?" Dagger asked.

"It's something called a season."

I turned around to see that Shira had joined us. She was watching us lovingly, and actually seemed pretty comfortable with the kittens inside the truck bed. "No one see us in here." she said.

"I know mom. So it was a good idea to come out here, right?" Hunter told her enthusiastically.

Shira smiled and nodded her head. "Yes." she agreed. "But you still need nap." She tried to be stern but her voice had lost its strictness. "Let's see your hunting pounce." she told him.

The kittens squeaked excitedly, and they all jostled to be the first to pounce.

"Hold on." I said. "One at a time. Hunter, you go first."

Hunter pushed his crowding brothers and sisters away, and awkwardly assumed what he thought was a good hunting crouch. I had to stifle a chuckle, and there were a lot of things I could have said, but I just smiled at Shira and kept my mouth shut. She was smiling too.

"Call that a hunting crouch?" Dagger crowed. "It looks like you're constipated."

Everybody laughed, and Hunter turned red. He steadied himself more, and leaped toward the box, landing squarely on top of it. He lifted his chin and glared at them challengingly. Everyone stopped laughing. I was quite impressed that even though the whole family laughed at him, he didn't give up, and he did a wonderful job.

"Let's see if you do better." Hunter meowed at Dagger. Dagger looked nervous.

After that, the truck bed became a great place for the kittens to play, and Shira liked it because it was safe.

****

Time past, and those times early were so awesome. The kittens grew fast, and Hunter showed all the signs of becoming a great hunter. When he caught his first mouse, we had a huge party for him.

For while, we had to be careful because there were humans around. But it was worth it because the restaurant garbage cans were always full of treats. But then, the people gradually stopped appearing, and the place became much more peaceful. We didn't miss the food so much because there were plenty of mice and birds around and the neighborhood was safer without all the people.

One day though, late in the winter, during a time when the snow was quite deep, we woke up to the sound of a loud roaring engine. Shira and I recognized the sound and the smell right away. We knew it was a big truck even before we saw it, and we wondered what it was doing in our peaceful back yard.

Shira stood up first, peering out the broken back window, and I joined her. Together we watched a huge, yellow tractor driving toward the building on the corner, near to where the alley turned in from the road. We were shocked to see it crash into the corner, knocking a huge chunk of the old restaurant down and sending a billowing cloud of dust out into the cold winter air.

We crouched down in surprise and alarm, shocked at the roaring sound, and all the kittens cried out together in fear. It was really loud, and the tractor started beeping piercingly as it backed out for another run.

We watched the entire building get destroyed, and we didn't know what it all meant, but once the first building was down, the truck turned up the alley and started on the next one, which was getting pretty close to where we were cowering in our uncertainty.

"What's happening?" Shira yowled, trying to be heard over the deafening noise. Her voice was filled with fear.

"It's time to move again." I answered with my heart beating in my throat. "It's not safe here anymore."

The kittens were all lying on the seat, with their paws over their ears. Only Hunter had the courage to venture up to watch the scene. Shira pushed him back down protectively without saying anything, and we continued to think about what we could do.

The yellow tractor had gotten really close, and the dust was making us cough. It was moving toward us, and there was no escape. With dismay, I realized that the tractor was going to smash down the fish shop that was right beside us. I figured Shira had realized the same thing.

"Run!!!" Shira screeched. The kittens flooded out of the truck, squawking in fear and confusion.

"Stop! We need to stay together!" I yelled, but no one listened. And I didn't blame them. Who would stop when they thought they might die?

Then I saw the big round ball that had smashed down the buildings was now aiming right for the truck. I jumped off before it hit me, the ball missing me just by an inch.

Our home fell down with a loud crash and a thud. That's when my family turned chaotic. They were running around everywhere, not sure where to go to get away. Even the brave Hunter was scared and out of control. I had to get my family to safety.

I spotted Shira limping as fast as she could. She was taking a path behind the tractor, and the kittens were following her. I sighed in relief that they were all together.

I ran toward them, but then, the tractor started going backwards, separating the family group. Shira, Nico, Dagger, and Echo were safe on the other side, Shira helping them to get out of the ally. But Hunter and Amber were in a very dangerous place.

The noise of the tractor was deafening, and it was too much for Amber, who crouched down in panic, unable to move. I ran back to save Hunter and Amber.

Hunter hadn't lost all of his courage. Before I got there he was able to dart across, avoiding the giant wheels. Amber watched him through squinting eyes. The she just squeezed them tightly shut and crouched even further down on her belly.

With a beeping sound, the tractor turned toward her, it's red light blazing like an evil monster's eye. I was almost there, but the ball smashed down into the wall that Amber was crouching under. I narrowed my eyes to spot her in the billowing dust.

"Amber!!" I screamed my lungs out in agony as the wall toppled down on top of her. There was no answer. I blindly ducked through the dust, coughing and sputtering. My stinging eyes searched rapidly for Amber's white and orange pelt.

Finally, I could see where she had been, but now, there was only a pile of rocks and bricks. I hurried toward it, totally forgetting about the tractor. I dug at the pile desperately, and finally found her body, all bloody and dusty. Her eyes were open and frozen in a scared, faraway look. She was dead, and there was nothing I could do.

Memories of Skipper dying flooded back. But this was much worse. She was my kitten. I sat down heavily beside her. A tear rolled down my cheek, and I sniffled and sobbed. I buried my nose in her dusty fur, trying to get her last sweet scent. For a moment, I didn't care whether I lived or died. But then, I thought of Shira and the other kittens waiting for me.

But, I wasn't going to let Amber's body get smashed and buried by bricks. I grabbed her by the scruff and heaved her toward safety.

The tractor hadn't given up yet though. It turned toward us again, raising the deadly black ball, ready to strike. Its huge black wheels were bearing down on me, and I had to save myself. But there was no way I could leap out of the way fast enough carrying Amber's limp body. It broke my heart to do it, but I had no choice but to drop her and get away.

Tears almost blinded me as I skirted around behind the devil tractor, and made my escape. The family was hiding behind a pile of wreckage outside of the range of the tractor.

When Shira spotted me, she ran toward me, brushing her head against my pelt, purring and examining me to make sure I was not hurt. But then she stopped, looking behind me as if she was expecting Amber to be standing there.

She didn't say anything at first, but only looked at me quizzically, and she could tell by the look of agony on my face that something horrible had happened to our daughter. Then, before I could think of anything appropriate to say, she turned away and fell into a sorrowful crouch, sobbing uncontrollably.

All of us gathered around her, sharing grief together, but then I had to speak. "We can't stay here." I told them. "Come on, Shira." I coaxed her gently. "We have to save the rest of our family, and we are not out of danger yet."

Shira could only follow me, and I was not sure where to go or what to do. I was so used to having her there with me, making plans together and courageously facing all of our challenges as a team. But she was too grief stricken to even care about anything, so I just lead the way.

Chapter 12

We kept walking and walking. There was no food, and the weather was freezing cold. There was no place to shelter. Whenever we thought we might have found a place, a defensive cat was already living there. We were too weak to fight, so we had to move on.

"How much longer Mom?" Hunter complained uncharacteristically, his voice shaking with the cold.

"Just a bit longer." Shira promised him. Shira and I exchanged looks. I really hoped what she said was true.

"My paws feel like they're coming off." Dagger whined.

"Yeah. I'm hungry and cold." Nico groaned beside his brother.

I knew we had to find a place to rest, even if it was only temporary. My eyes scanned the area surrounding us.

Usually we would have looked for an old building with someplace to hide, but we were in an area that didn't have any place good like that. There were only roads, big tall buildings, and sidewalks, so we had to think of something else.

"Look over here dad." Echo said, scurrying down the sidewalk and beside the curb. She was nosing into a broken metal cover over a hole that went under the sidewalk.

"That's a storm sewer." Hunter said authoritatively. "Mom showed me one of those when we were home."

His face saddened as he talked about home, and I felt a pang of sorrow too. A flash of Amber's joyful face crossed my memory. The old truck had been a wonderful place to live.

"We can squeeze in there for a while and at least get out of the weather." Shira suggested, moving forward. "Let me go first, in case there is something dangerous down there."

"Rats?" Dagger squeaked in a fearful voice.

"That's food." Hunter said bravely. "Me and father can kill a rat if we hunt together.

I didn't say anything, but I pushed quietly in front of Shira and entered into the darkness. My eyes adjusted quickly, and the first thing I noticed was a lot of trash lying on ground. It smelled really moldy and wet. The ground was cold, and my paws felt like blocks of ice, but at least there was no wind and snow. It was a place where the family could cuddle together, and share some body warmth. Every time a car passed, the roar of it echoed in the sewer.

Shira crowded in beside me. The kittens followed her, their noses twitching nervously. "I think we can shelter here for the night." I said.

"Eww." Nico cried, his nose wrinkling in distaste. "Shelter *here*? This place is gross!"

"Would you rather sleep out there?" Shira hissed impatiently, pointing her ears outside. The wind howled through the opening trying to get inside, and a dusting of snow filtered through.

"No, mom." Nico sighed. "I'm sorry. I'm just cold and hungry."

"We all are." I told them gently. "You guys group together into the corner there and get warm. I'm going for food."

Hunter's ears pricked up at the thought of hunting, but he didn't offer to come, and I didn't wait. The storm drains were part of a big system of tunnels, and I thought that would be a good place to hunt. I hoped there were mice, and no rats, but I thought I could take a rat if it wasn't too big.

"I'll be back soon." I said, and slipped away around the corner and out of sight.

The tunnels were dark, but every once in a while, light from outside would come streaming down from an opening above. I knew I could find my way back by following my own scent trail. A couple of times, I smelled prey, but the odor was faint, and not fresh, so I plodded on, desperate to find some food for my family.

Finally, after hunting for more than two hours, I caught the smell of a rat ahead. I had smelled one before, but had passed it hoping for a less dangerous hunt. Since then it had grown darker, and the cold night was approaching.

Desperation made me willing to take the risk.

I stalked the rat stealthily, and after a few moments I sensed that he was aware of me. I couldn't see him yet, but he had quickened his pace. Coming around a bend in the tunnel, I realized that it was a dead end, and a large, red eyed rodent crouched there at the end, looking at me with hatred, and the glare of battle in his eyes.

I almost let out of yelp of surprise as the rat streaked past me, rustling the leaves. But I couldn't give up and go back to my family empty handed. How disappointed they would be

I had to move fast, and I twisted, giving chase and trying to grab him with my claws. He had a head start, but I was only a whisker away from him the whole time. Finally, just before he disappeared into a small hole, I caught a hold of his long, naked, pink tail, barely hooking it with only one claw.

The rat screeched and struggled wildly, but I pulled him closer, and got a better hold of him. That's when he turned into a wild demon. With a strange battle cry, it jumped straight in my face, scratching me, trying to blind my eyes. I hissed and backed away, but I couldn't take my claws off that stinking rat's tail.

I spun my arms and the rat spun too, it's narrow eyes rolling in confusion. The rat was off balance, but I wasn't. So I planted my feet, and swung him sideways with all my strength. He was big, but it was enough to smash him on the wall.

The rat fell to the ground dazed. Before he could recover and run away, I pounced clumsily, trying not to hit the ceiling, and sunk my teeth down into its back wrenching sideways violently and breaking its spine.

When I carried it to the kittens, they stared at me with admiration, and begged me to tell the story of how I caught it.

A rat wasn't enough to fill all our bellies, but every one of us got a few mouthfuls and it was a lot better than nothing.

The rat didn't taste good. It had nasty, stringy fur. The meat was tough and it tasted a bit bitter.

When we were all done, we snuggled up in a corner where the wall could block the wind. We had gathered a pile of leaves together for a bed. We were all shivering in the cold, and we all pressed ourselves closer to get warmer.

Time passed, but I had trouble going to sleep. The kittens were all snoring loudly after their long tired journey, but I kept thinking about what we were going to do when the next day came.

I decided that I should go get some fresh air, and quietly tiptoed to the opening, not wanting to wake up Shira and the kittens.

I sighed, looking up at the night sky, wanting to see the twinkling stars like I had seen them on the ship. But I could only see one lonely star, barely visible because of the city lights.

I wrapped my tail around my paws and sat there thinking about my life. I wished to go back to my early life with Terrah, when everything was safe and I had no worries. I wondered what would have happened if I hadn't jumped out of the car, didn't meet Skipper, and didn't meet Shira. I had all my attention on my own thinking, and I didn't notice that Shira was coming out of the opening.

"Hey." Shira said sitting next to me.

"Hey." I replied back, still deep in my own thoughts.

"What are you doing out here?" She asked. Her soft words were almost drowned out by the sound of a passing car.

I took a deep breath and scooted over bit so that we were touching comfortingly. "I was thinking about tomorrow and what we should do." I told her.

"Me too." Shira answered, looking troubled. "I couldn't sleep. Do you have any ideas about our situation?"

"We can't stay here." I told her. "It's too hard to find food, and it's too dangerous." As I spoke, another car flashed past us, the wind of it blowing our fur. "I didn't tell you, but that rat almost got the better of me."

She didn't answer, and I knew how much she wished that we could hunt together, so I didn't pursue that thought. "We need to find some breakfast and then move on as soon as we can. There has to be someplace better than this."

She agreed, and purred an encouraging purr That small sound meant a lot to me. "Tell you what." I said. "Tomorrow, I'll take Hunter to get some breakfast, and then you and I can go look for a better place to stay."

We sat there for a while, feeling better. Suddenly Shira coughed loudly.

"Are you okay?" I asked her, feeling worried.

"Yeah, I'm fine. Just a hairball stuck in my throat." Shira answered in a scratchy voice.

I looked at her anxiously. That wasn't a hairball cough. If she stayed up here in the cold any longer, she might be sick.

"Come on." I told her. 'Let's go back down and get some sleep."

****

I was the first one awake the next morning. Shira was still sleeping soundly. I guessed it was because she was tired after our midnight talk, although she was usually the first one awake.

"Get up." I whispered, nudging Hunter. Hunter groaned and drool dropped from his mouth.

"Blah." He grumbled.

"We're going hunting." I told him.

Hunter opened his eyes at the word, 'hunting'. He yawned, and got up, stretching his body. He looked around, and when he saw that everyone else was sleeping, he tiptoed over to me, and whispered excitedly. "Let's go!"

The morning air was especially cold. It had stopped snowing and the sun was shining through the grate. Leaving the warmth of the family sleeping pile was hard and we both shivered.

"Brr…" Hunter growled. "I don't really like rat meat. Can we hunt something else?"

"I doubt it." I sighed. "Rats are the only things down here. I guess there might be birds outside, but it's too dangerous."

Hunter shrugged. "Then I guess we have no choice."

We worked well together, and I was proud of Hunter. He was really growing up fast. I taught him the scent of rat, and the difference between a fresh trail and an old trail. He learned fast, and I let him follow the scent first when we found a hot one. It led into a smaller branch of the tunnels until we saw up ahead, in the semi-darkness, a pile of old rags and papers. The smell was strong there. It was a rat nest.

Hunter crouched down, silent and intent, and I slipped silently up beside him. "You circle around to the side of the nest, and I will come in from behind him." I directed. "Do you want to make the first pounce?" I asked. "I'll be right there if anything goes wrong."

"Really?" Hunter meowed excitedly. "Do you think I can do it?"

"The rat is in his nest, so we'll totally surprise him. Just do it like I taught you and get him quickly behind the neck, where he can't turn on you with his teeth and claws."

Hunter fidgeted for a moment, considering. "Got it." He finally said with determination in his voice.

I watched him work his way stealthily into position, and then creep silently closer and closer to the target. I snuck closer myself until I was just behind the nest, and I could see the tail and the hump of the rat's grayish brown back.

I sensed that it was a big rat and worried a little. But now was as good a time as any for Hunter to learn. The rat was right in front of me, totally unaware of his danger. My paws itched to pounce and kill this rat myself, but I had already decided to let Hunter try.

I caught Hunter's eye. As soon as I nodded to him, he leaped perfectly, landing on the rat's back. It squealed in surprise and alarm, but since Hunter was on its back, it could do nothing to get free. Hunter gave it a quick deadly bite on the back of its neck, and it was over.

He grabbed the rat in his jaws, and lifted his chin proudly. I gaped. "You-Were-Amazing!" I purred loudly, rubbing myself against him.

Hunter purred too. "I was, wasn't I?" He mewed pride shining in his eyes.

"Of course!" I exclaimed. "Rats are really hard to catch, but you did it so easily! Your mother is going to be really proud of you."

When we got back to where we slept, Dagger, Nico, and Echo were play-fighting squealing happily. They bounced toward us when they spotted us.

"We wondered where you went!" Echo said. She stopped when she saw the rat hanging from Hunter's mouth. "Wow." She breathed. "Did *you* catch that?"

Hunter nodded. "Yup. All by myself." He boasted, and the kittens crowded near him to hear the story.

I figured Shira would lick Hunter, congratulating him, telling him what a good hunter he was. But she didn't. She was still sleeping. A bad, uneasy feeling creped through my pelt. I padded over to her.

"Shira, wake up." I said, prodding her gently with my paw. That's when I noticed that her coat was hot and she was sweating. I knew something was wrong.

"Shira!" I said more loudly, shaking her. Shira opened her emerald eyes slowly and groaned.

"Feel… so… sick…" She moaned.

"I know." I said licking her fur soothingly. "You're going to be all right."

She moaned again. I knew that this wasn't a good place to shelter. We had to find a good warm spot for Shira.

"I'll go out and look for a place we can stay." I told her. "You stay here and watch the kittens."

"But... you said... together..." She mewed, breaking off with a cough.

"Yes, I know..." I said desperately. "But you're too sick. What if something happens to you? Think about the kittens."

Shira sighed, then collapsed to the floor coughing and moaning. I hated to leave her alone with the kittens like this, but the sooner we found a good place to stay, the better.

Hunter was busy telling the story, bluffing a bit. "...and the rat tried to run away, but I was too fast for it! Before it could get away, I held him down, and we wrestled like crazy. The rat's eyes were glaring at me like it wanted to eat *me*!" The other kittens gasped and looked frightened.

I nosed Hunter. "I'm going to go look for a good place for us to stay. I need you to look after everyone. Keep and eye on your mother too. She's sick." I told him.

Hunter looked worried, but he kept his brave face. "You can count on me, Dad." He meowed.

I knew I could count on him. I nodded and went out to the road.

Chapter 13

It hadn't warmed up, even though the sun was shining on the snow, and it hurt my eyes after being underground. My first thought was to get away from all these streets, and I needed to get to a higher place so that I could see far enough to pick a good direction to try.

There was a little hill off in the distance, and I could see a tree on the top of it, so I decided to try that way. I set off toward it, crossing the road. I guess it was too early for many cars because I only had to wait a short time before I could cross.

It took some time of uneventful walking before I got to the hill. There was a fence around the bottom of it, but I could easily squeeze through it, so it wasn't long before I was headed upwards through the bushes and the trees.

There were a bunch of old cars lying around, and I smelled the dog before it saw me. It had that dirty dog stink when the animal got wet but never took a bath. I hated that smell, but I was hopeful, because he might be able to help me find out about this place if he was nice. I decided to scout around and see if I could find him. It didn't take long.

He was a brown and white bulldog. He had a very mean look, and drool dropped from his mouth. I gulped. Maybe I shouldn't talk to him at all. But I was here already, and it was too late to turn back. The bull dog turned, and saw me.

"Uh, Hello." I said awkwardly. "Could you be kind enough to tell me where I can find a warm place to stay?"

"No." The dog growled. "Get out of here before I tear your guts out, and have them for lunch."

I realized that he was serious. But who knew? There might be a very good place here, and the dog might be hiding it. Besides, I needed to look around from on top of the hill. I glanced around, pretended that he won, and I started slinking away.

A second later, I ran as fast as I could toward the hilltop. As I passed the dog I saw his eyes so full of malice. "Sucker!" I yowled, thinking the dog was leashed and he couldn't get me.

I felt hot breath on my tail, and I turned my head around to see the dog, hot on my trail.

I was surprised and horrified, but I didn't really have time to think about it.

His mouth was so big it could eat me in one bite, and he was faster than he looked on his short, fat legs.

"Die cat!" he growled threateningly, and his teeth snapped with sickening power just an inch from the end of my tail. I desperately scanned the area for a place to hide, and spotted an old blue car all smashed up and rusty. The door was open a little, and I darted through it, thinking he couldn't fit in after me. But I was wrong.

It didn't cross my mind to look at the broken windows, and he leaped up, barreling through, and landing on the seat right beside me. In a panic, I slipped around between the door and the seat, trying to avoid him by getting in the back.

The dog tried to follow me, pushing against the door, which only moved a little bit, and when he did it, his head got inside the seat belt, and the door pushed him tight against the seat. That is when he really went psycho, thrashing around with frightening strength, barking and growling like a monster all the while.

I felt it was all over for me, and I cowered in the corner, squeezing my eyes shut, all my family's faces flashing though my mind. But the chomp of his yellow teeth never came, and I opened one eye for a peep to see what was going on.

He was stuck, and his struggles were just making it worse. I heaved a huge sigh of relief, and ventured forward, taking a seat just out of reach of him. I sat there, licking my paw, trying to look composed, and he glared at me hatefully.

"You think you're safe?" he asked me. "Wait till I get outta here!" he threatened, going into another spasm of rage and struggle.

I just watched him for a minute, and then said, "I can get you out, but you have to promise you'll help me."

Those words made him stop and look at me with his big red eyes. "You've gotta be kidding me." He growled, but some of the menace had gone out of his tone.

I just looked at him as if he was one of my kittens. "You are having a bad day, and you're a bit grouchy today." I said understandingly. "It happens to all of us, but I think you are probably not normally like this, so I can help you out, I guess." I didn't know if my tactics would work, but it was worth a try.

"I have a family." I told him. "I need a warm place to shelter for awhile, and I'm not from around here. All you have to do is tell me what you know. Then I will help you out of that ridiculous situation."

He thought about it for a minute, and then said. "Yeah. It's a bad day, and it just got worse. Sorry I was such a grouch." His right foot was stuck awkwardly upward and poked out above his head. "I think I might know a place that you could hang out for a while."

My eyes gleamed, and my heart pounded harder, but I knew I had to keep my composure to control this situation, so I just looked at him and nodded. "Go on." I said.

"Well, if you go to the other side of my hill, and you go for about another five or ten minutes, you will come to a human place where they live. There are a lot of good food smells around there, and not many cars. I've been there a couple of times, and I always see fat, happy cats around there. Why don't you check it out?" he concluded.

I considered his words, wondering if he was being sincere, or if he would kill me when I tried to help him. "How do I know you are telling the truth?" I asked, licking my paw again as though I were in complete control of my feelings.

"You have my word." He said. "And if you don't find a place, you can come back here and sleep in one of my cars." He told me sheepishly, obviously desperate to get free.

I decided to trust him and moved forward toward his right shoulder, where the seatbelt had looped around him and was trapping him. His breath smelled like a mix of meat and drool, and I had to hide my disgust. Actually, in that first second or two, I wasn't sure if he would bite my head off, but fortunately, he didn't.

I had to push up against him to hook the belt with my claws, and I was able to inch it forward. I gave him instructions to move this way and that way, which he obeyed well. It took about 5 minutes, but finally he was able to break free, and he wriggled his fat, muscular body backwards and pushed his way out of car.

"My name is Bruiser." He said, as if I really cared. He waited awkwardly for me to tell him my name, so I told him the same thing I had told Skipper, and thinking of my old friend brought some softness to my heart, even for this big brute.

Chapter 14

After we said our goodbyes, I headed down the hill. I was surprised at how different it was on the other side. Instead of huge high buildings, there were many houses like the one me and Terrah used to live in a long, long time ago. It actually felt cozy.

'Maybe Terrah's somewhere here?' I thought, but quickly pushed the idea away. New York was a humongous city, and she could be anywhere. How do I even know if Terrah still lives here? I didn't want to get my hopes up and

be disappointed. Besides, I have a great life with my family.

I stepped into the neighborhood. There were not so many cars on the street, and there were many trees. Snow covered the lawns in the human's yards. I saw a white, fluffy cat sitting on a porch, enjoying the fresh air.

Of course I know about cat's territories, and how they don't want unfamiliar strangers there. So I went to the edge of her yard, and called out to her.

She jumped when she saw me, her fur bristling defensively and her tail arched. She hissed when I took a step closer.

I blinked slowly and sat down to show her I meant no harm. She relaxed a little, but she was poised to run away if I moved any closer.

"You're a stray." She meowed. "I don't want your dirty paws on my place."

"Okay." I said. "I'll be gone if you tell me one thing."

"What?" She asked tentatively.

"Nothing bad." I promised her. "Just tell me where I can spend a night around here. I have kittens, and their mother is very sick."

"Oh." She said looking relived. She thought a little. "You see that house over there?" She said, pointing her nose at a blue-gray house.

I nodded.

"The humans there are on vacation. I guess you can shelter in that garage for a couple days until they get back." She said.

I dipped my head thankfully. "Thanks a million." I said.

"You're welcome." She called as I padded away to investigate the house.

There was a little doggy door in the garage, and I was able to push through it and go into the big, dim room. The light from outside was shining through a small window, and although it was still cold, it was quite a bit warmer than it was outside.

There was a freezer beside the stairs going up into the house, and I recognized it from my days stealing food with Skipper. I tried the door, and it popped open under my expert paws. I could smell the meat, and although I knew it would be hard as a rock, I also knew that it would soften and be delicious if we left it out on the floor for a while. I had seen enough.

The journey back to the sewers was interrupted by the traffic again, and I had to hide out, waiting until quite late for the cars to thin out. With nothing to do but worry all that time, I was really concerned by the time I got back, well after dark.

I was right to be upset, because Shira was worse. Not only that, but now, Dagger was coughing, and his nose was hard and dry, like cats get when they are sick.

Hunter was sitting with them, his paw up on his mother's neck comfortingly. "I'm sorry Dad." He told me mournfully. "I didn't know what to do."

"It's not your fault." I reassured him, patting him gently on the shoulder with my tail.

Hunter sighed, then sat down as I padded over to Shira and Dagger.

"Hi...Dad..." Dagger meowed, his voice croaking.

"Hey." I greeted him. I tried my best to act normal, like nothing was wrong.

"Is Dagger gonna die?" Echo mewed fearfully.

"No." I said softly. "He just caught a cold. No one's gonna die." I hoped that was true.

"Are mom and Dagger okay?" Nico asked. "Are we going to catch it too?"

"Not if you stay away." I told him as gently as I could. "Can I have a moment with your mother?"

"Okay." Hunter meowed, then hesitated. "What about Dagger?" He asked.

I glanced at Dagger, who seemed so small, and fragile. He coughed and sniffed. "Dagger can stay here." I said. Hunter nodded, and led Nico, and Echo away.

"Shira." I said. She looked at me her eyes filled with sorrow.

"It's all... my fault." She sniffled. "Because of me... Dagger got sick too..."

"No." I mewed. "It's not your fault. Some things just happen. No one is to blame. "

Shira said nothing, looking far away.

"Listen." I said, changing the subject. "There's a place I found. It's warm, but it's quite far away. Can you walk that far?"

"Yes." She said immediately. "Let's go."

"What? Now?" I meowed, surprised.

"Yes. Anywhere's good if it's away from here." Shira mewed, and struggled to get on her paws.

"All right..." I said. "We'll support Dagger on the way."

I called the kittens. They all seemed eager to get out of that place, so we started off.

When we got to the hill with one tree on it, Shira was too sick to continue and collapsed onto the ground, coughing and groaning.

My eyes searched rapidly for Bruiser. Finally, I spotted his dog house, and hurried over to it. He was sleeping, snoring loudly. I poked his fat arm.

Bruiser jumped up, growling. He stopped when he saw me. "Oh. It's you." He said sitting down. "What are you doing here at night?"

"My wife and kittens are here, and they're sick. They need somewhere to rest before we move on." I explained, looking at him pleadingly.

"Fine." Bruiser grunted. "I guess you can rest in one of my cars. Just be careful not to get caught."

"Thank you, thank you!" I meowed to him, and went to Shira.

We picked a truck that looked a lot like the one we used to live in. We gave Shira and Dagger the most warm and comfortable seat, and we all immediately went to sleep, exhausted.

Dawn came around, and sun appeared through the buildings. It was still cold, but better compared to the cold windy weather we had experienced here so far. Snow began to melt. It was a good sign. Spring would be here soon.

Shira was a lot better when we woke up. She still coughed, but now her dizziness and tiredness seemed to have eased.

However, Dagger was worse. He was coughing more than ever and he's pelt was really hot. He moaned the whole time, and barely managed to speak.

"Dad, I'm hungry." Echo complained. "Can we go for a quick hunt?"

I realized then that my stomach was growling with hunger. We hadn't eaten since yesterday morning and I knew starving the sick cats wasn't a good idea.

"Okay." I agreed. "But I don't think there will be any prey here. Let's go look in the trash."

Echo volunteered to look after Dagger with Shira, so Hunter and Nico tagged along with me to look for food.

We snuck to the bottom of the hill and through the fence. It didn't take long to find a trashcan nearby. It was full. I figured it was because humans lived around here.

Nico jumped right into the trashcan. A moment later, he appeared with a piece of pizza in his mouth.

"I don't know what this is, but it smells like food." He announced. Hunter trotted over to him to have a sniff.

"It's great!" I told him. "But it's not enough. Let's look for more."

I searched behind the trashcan while Nico joined Hunter inside to look. I turned around when I heard noises inside.

"Hey!"

"Get off, you lump!"

"I found it first!"

"I *grabbed* it first!"

It was Hunter who poked his head out first. He had something in his mouth. It was a half-eaten chicken.

"Great job!" I meowed. "I think that'll be enough."

Nico glared at Hunter. "I found it first." He growled.

"Did not."

"Did too."

"Enough, boys." I sighed. But inside I was snickering in amusement.

With Nico carrying the pizza, and Hunter carrying the chicken, we headed back to the others. Nico and Hunter were racing to see who could get back faster.

Something caught my eye as I followed along. It was a pigeon feather. *'The kittens will love that.'* I smiled to myself. *'Too bad Dagger's not well enough to play yet.'* I thought sadly.

We all shared the food, and it was gone in a flash, except what we left for Dagger. He was sleeping, and we didn't want to wake him. I licked my lips, wanting to get the last taste. Hunter chewed on the chicken bone as if he was too miserable that the food was gone already.

I took the feather I had collected on the way back, and blew it up into the air. The cold wind caught it, and carried it past the kittens. As I had expected, they all leaped into the air, trying to catch it. Shira and I watched side by side in satisfaction.

"I really hope Dagger gets well soon." Shira sighed.

I nodded. "Yeah...But spring's just around the corner. I'm sure he'll be better."

Chapter 15

It was getting late, and Dagger was still sleeping. We hated to disturb him from his peaceful sleep, since he was sick, but we had to get a move on.

Shira and I went over to him. "Dagger, honey, it's time to wake up. We need to go to our new, warm temporary home, and you can sleep there as long as you please." Shira said prodding him softly with her paw.

Dagger didn't even budge. And Shira looked at me with anxious expression.

"Dagger!" I tried, shaking him. He's body was stiff and cold. My heart pounding, I bent over to check his heart beat, but I already knew it was too late.

"No…" Shira sobbed. "It's all my fault! It should have been me instead of Dagger!"

"What's wrong?" Echo said, poking her head between us. Her face got rigid when she saw Dagger's body, and she broke into a high pitched wail.

The other kittens came to us at the sound of Echo's cry. "No!!!" Nico whimpered. "Not Dagger too…"

Hunter sat there, his head hung low. Echo tried to run and bury her face in Dagger's lifeless fur, but I held her back.

I waited patiently while the family mourned. When enough time had passed, I urged everyone to go outside, while I decided what to do with

Dagger's body. I picked him up as gently as I could and carried him out the other door of the truck so that the others couldn't see me. It was a short distance into the forest, and I laid him there in a hollow under the roots of a tree where I thought he would lie undisturbed and in peace forever. Then I went back to what was left of my family.

Bruiser was there, and Shira was standing protectively between him and the kittens. "It's okay." I told her. "You can trust him." But she only hissed and raised her neck hairs.

"That's fine." Bruiser said, smiling and slobbering at the same time. "I don't like cats either, but with you it's a special case." He told me. "You have to get outta sight though." He continued. "The humans will come pretty soon."

"Thank you, Bruiser." I told him with a tired voice. "We have to go now anyway."

He came with us as we made our way down to the other fence, and got right up close to me when he said goodbye. "You are welcome to come back if you need too." He whispered, his meaty dog breath wafting over me.

"I appreciate that Bruiser." I told him, trying not to breathe. "I found an unexpected friend here, and I will always remember you that way." Then I turned away, and we moved on toward the new neighborhood off in the distance.

Shira was still coughing, but she was stronger, and the second part of our journey went pretty well. The kittens had never been in a human's neighborhood before, and they were wide eyed and excited about living there. I didn't have the heart to tell them that we could only stay a couple of days. I would save that news for later.

The white cat was watching us out the window as we crossed the street toward the house with the garage, and our eyes met for a moment before she turned away, showing snobbish indifference. I stood outside while the rest of the family pushed the swinging door aside, and entered the garage.

The first order of business was to get a nice bed where Shira could rest and stay warm. We found a soft blanket on some shelves. It was big enough for all five of us, so we jumped up there and settled down very comfortably. I could even see out the window and get a view of the driveway from there.

Soon though, I jumped down and padded over to the freezer. I leaped deftly up and popped open the door. It was cold inside and it froze my feet, but I was able to find a big frozen salmon, and I dragged it out onto the floor.

It landed with a thud, like a brick, and it was as hard as a rock. But experience had taught me that I only had to wait for it to get warm, soft, and delicious. It turned out to be a wonderful meal.

We all rested again after eating, and our bellies were fat and round for the first time in a long while. But I knew we couldn't stay, so while the kittens were sleeping soundly, Shira and I had a serious talk.

"The humans who live here will be back soon." I told her. "That 'stuck up' pet told me that we only have a few days until they come back."

Shira sighed and shook her head, and with a weary resignation, suggested that I go out and scout for a more permanent home.

I stood and stretched, preparing myself for another adventure.

I went out the doggy door we had used to get in. I made my way through the neighborhood, checking every place that could be safe and long-term.

I crossed a bunch of streets and saw some unfriendly pets.

"Get out of my lawn." One of them hissed. What was more distressing was that I wasn't even in his lawn! I was just on the side walk. However, I was not looking for a fight.

"Mind your own business." I growled, and kept on moving. I hadn't realized how prejudice pets were toward strays, and I didn't like the idea of my kittens being treated like this. But if there was one thing I had learned, it was that the world is not a fair place.

The next block I came to, had no houses on it, but only low rows of brick buildings with big windows on the front. It was a rather busy place, with people walking along the sidewalks and carrying shopping bags. It might be a place where we could find food in the garbage cans behind the stores, and there were a few pets in the area too. I decided to scout around a little bit more.

I was just getting ready to duck around a corner and go into a back alley when a familiar odor hit me in the face like truck. It was the smell of sweet apples, just like Terrah.

I raised my head, and saw a young woman carrying a bag of groceries. She had tan skin, and cacao brown eyes. She looked a lot like Terrah.

I blinked. I suddenly realized the apple scent was coming from her, and that *she* was Terrah!

I stood there, frozen. *'What do I do now?'* Terrah was getting on her bike. She slipped the grocery bag on the handle, and the bike started to move.

My mind whirled like a tornado. I wasn't going to lose her again like I did long ago. But what about Shira and the kittens? What if I got lost following her?

The bike was starting to gain speed. I started running too. My legs were just moving without even thinking. I didn't have time to think. Soon, I was chasing after that bicycle as fast as I could run.

Wind brushed my fur, and I had to narrow my eyes to see. It was hard, because I had to dodge around humans' legs. Some people yowled and pointed at me, but I didn't bother to look at them. I didn't want to lose her this time, so I didn't take my eyes off her.

A few minutes past, and we were still running. I huffed and puffed to catch up. I was getting pretty tired, and I longed to sit down for a minute.

Finally, the bike slowed down and stopped. I sighed, breathing heavily as I watched Terrah get off the bike and head into a gray roofed house. She didn't see me.

I started to follow her, but then I stopped. What about Shira and the kittens? That house didn't have a doggy door. If I went in, I might not be able to get back out again.

I decided to bring my family here. Terrah would take them in. I closed my eyes, and opened my mouth, letting the scents flow in. I wanted to remember this house. It smelled of peppermint and sweet apples, like Terrah.

"I'll come back." I said to myself, and to Terrah, even though she couldn't hear me.

I didn't remember how long I had followed her, and I was sure I didn't want to forget how to come back with my family, so I paused and began looking around at the landmarks in the neighborhood. That is when I saw the calico female cat sitting on the fence. She had been watching me, and her ears were back against her head in a hostile, unwelcoming posture.

Thinking that she was going to be my neighbor, I paused to be friendly. "Hello." I said nicely.

The calico cat glared at me and hissed. I cocked my head in surprise as two other cats leaped to her side.

One was copper colored tom, and the other was a black and white tuxedo cat.

"Strays aren't welcome here." The copper tom growled in a husky voice. He seemed to be the boss. "This is our territory."

"I was just passing through." I explained. "I mean no harm." I took a step toward the gap between the cats to get out of there, but the black cat blocked my way.

"Oh, we saw you following that human. Do you think you can come back here?" He snarled.

I gulped. The cats surrounded me, their eyes flashing menacingly. "Let's give him something he'll never forget." The calico cat jeered.

"Yeah..." The black cat snickered. "...or, maybe, he'll *never* come back."

"Let's make his death *slow*." The copper cat smiled viciously.

I bristled, looking around for a way out. But it was pretty dismal. I realized it was fight, or die.

They were circling me. I flattened my ears, and hissed, but they only laughed.

I don't remember who it was, but one of them barreled into me, knocking my breath out. I gasped, and raked his face. He flinched, but I couldn't follow through with him because the other two had piled on me.

One of them bit me on the back leg, and I hissed in agony. I could feel the blood pouring out.

Growling in anger, I swatted powerfully at the calico cat. My paw slashed across her eyes, and she howled painfully backing away.

I was hurt, but I could still defend myself. I pounced on the copper tom, wrestling. He batted me on the face, making my nose bleed. I clawed him back on the shoulder shredding skin and muscle under my outstretched talons. He hissed, and tried to back away, but I pushed him back down.

I was about to finish him, when the black tom came to his rescue. He knocked me off, and we exchanged a couple of blows. Suddenly, he twisted his head, and bit me hard on the neck. I yowled as the pain rushed in. I wanted to scream, but he was holding my throat. The others came, their eyes filled with revenge and hatred.

The calico cat leaped in, pushing the black cat away, and struck my stomach with full strength. I gasped and gagged. I tried to stand up, but I couldn't move.

"Prepare to die." The copper tom hissed as he bared his teeth to finish me.

I closed my eyes, waiting for the fatal bite and pain to crash in. I thought about how close I was to getting back to Terrah, and how happy I was with Shira and the kittens. Maybe I'll find Amber and Dagger when I die.

However, the pain never came. Instead, I heard the door of the house slam, and a human voice shouting. We had been making a lot of noise, and someone had heard us. Cautiously, I opened my eyes. I saw Terrah running over to us and shooing my enemies away.

The copper tom glared at me as he turned around. "You are *so* lucky." He growled as he ran after the others. "We'll finish you next time."

I saw Terrah bend over to me to check if I was okay. I purred weakly at her touch as she lifted me up. Her eyes shone as recognized me.

"Kitty...?" She asked with an incredulous tone. "How did you find me after all these years?" I tried my best to meow back to her, but I blacked out.

Chapter 16

When I opened my eyes, I found myself in a living room. But one sniff of the air told me that it was Terrah's house. I looked at my body. It was covered in blood soaked bandages.

'How did I get here?' I thought. Then I remembered and I stood up, painfully. Terrah was sitting on a sofa, reading magazines, and looked up when she saw me.

"Oh! You're awake, Kitty!" She smiled at me. "You slept all the time at the vet. Should I get you some milk and tuna?"

I blinked. It was so great to hear her voice again. "Yes, please." I purred. Hearing her talk made me forget all my injuries, and I limped over to her. I rubbed myself at her leg, letting her scent wash over me. She laughed and stroked my fur.

As she walked toward the kitchen, I followed her awkwardly with my tight bandages making it hard to move freely. All those years of anger and frustration toward her melted away, and I only felt the old love and happiness that we used to have.

But there was a nagging worry in my heart. *'What about Shira and the kittens?'* I thought, knowing that I had to go back as soon as I could. *'How worried they would be.'* I hoped this was not a dream, and I could unite my family and Terrah in a safe, happy home together.

I was eating voraciously, surprised at how hungry I was. But even so, my mind was focused on getting my family here.

It was morning time, and it seemed as though I had slept through the night. Terrah was putting on her lipstick, and then her coat. She came to me and kneeled down beside me, petting me as I drank my milk. "I have to go to work, Kitty." She said apologetically. "My boss will be angry if I'm late. Just rest and I'll be home later." Then she stood, and I sat watching her as she left through the back door.

I limped to the living room and jumped up on to the back of the sofa where I could watch her as she backed her car out of the driveway and disappeared down the road.

I took that as my cue and limped toward the open window. In the old days, Terrah's family had always left the window open for me, and this was just like old times.

Leaping out onto the ground was a painful experience, and I was fearful that the neighborhood cats would see me and come to finish me off. So I slinked around behind bushes, and used parked cars and other hiding places until I was out of the area.

It took me a long time to travel all the way back to the garage, and I was in a lot of pain by the time I got there. My leg had started bleeding again, and my bandage had fallen off, exposing an area around the wound where the vet had shaved off my hair. I stopped occasionally to lick the deep gash and to clean the dried blood off the stitches that the doctor had sewn into my flesh.

When I finally arrived, I could see the kittens and Shira sitting out under the bushes beside the driveway. I saw them first, and a pang of relief flooded in.

Shira spotted me, and raced toward me. "Where have you been?" She demanded. She examined me. "And what *happened* to you?"

"Sorry." I mewed. "I had a fight with these strange cats and couldn't get away. I found a place to stay though."

Shira ignored me. "Do you know how *worried* we were? Hunter went out looking for you! And what if the humans came back when you were away?"

I whimpered. "I'm really sorry." I apologized. "Where's Hunter?"

"He's not back yet." Shira said more calmly this time. She glanced at my leg. "Ooh! You're like me now!"

I purred. Shira came over to sniff my leg. She looked at me with surprise and disapproval.

"We need to talk." I said knowing that Shira smelled Terrah's scent on me.

I saw Echo and Nico hurry toward me. "Dad!" They called. "You'll back!"

I purred. Shira pushed me to the corner. "Please tell me that this place you found doesn't have any human involved." She growled. "I have a *nose*, you know. I can smell human all over you."

"This *'human'* saved my life." I argued. "And she happens to be my owner from before."

"That *'human'* abandoned you." She countered forcefully. "How can you trust her now?"

"That was an accident." I sniffed. The old doubts were creeping back, but I shook my head. "Remember Pete?" I said. "He was nice. Terrah is too. You can't think that all humans are bad."

Shira looked uncertain. "Pete was different."

"And what about Bruiser?" I reasoned. "You thought every dog was bad. But he helped us."

Shira glanced away, not meeting my eyes. Just then Hunter appeared from around the corner.

"Dad!" He meowed happily. "You came back! I was looking for you!"

"Shh." Echo whispered. "Mom and dad are *fighting*."

"We lost two of our kittens already." I said softly. "If we stay there, Terrah will help us protect them. Let's at least try. Terrah leaves the window open. We can get in and out whenever we please."

Shira thought for a moment. "Fine." She growled. "But I'm not promising I'll stay there."

I purred. "Thank you."

"Wow! We're gonna stay in a human's house!" Nico shouted.

"Cool!" Hunter chimed in. "Is that house like this one?"

"A lot better." I promised. "Let's go now before Terrah comes back. She might wonder where I went."

Shira narrowed her eyes at me, but she said nothing. *'I'm sure Shira willlike Terrah.'* I told myself, not quite convinced, but I was very determined nonetheless.

We were getting pretty close now, and the kittens were all excited. I limped along, leading the way when suddenly, a familiar snarl sounded in my ear. "Well, well, well. Look who came back." I turned around. It was the copper colored tom. The calico cat, and the tuxedo cat were with him.

"You got lucky last time, but now there's no one to save you." He jeered as they circled us.

I growled, and my family all clustered around me. Hunter, Shira and I were on the outside making a circle around Nico and Echo in the middle.

The copper color tom leaped straight for me. I leaped too, and met him in midair, both of us crashing down in twisting, whirling flurry of rage. I knew some of his tricks now, and rolled out of the way as he tried to trap me.

In the corner of my eye, I saw Hunter wrestling with the calico cat. Shira was fighting the black tom.

I ducked just in time to dodge the next blow, but felt the tip of my ear being torn. I hissed, and slammed my paw down onto my enemy's eye.

The calico now had Hunter pinned down, and I raced over to help him, smashing the calico cat off balance. Clapping my teeth under her throat, I pierced her skin and almost tore her life away. But at that moment I saw terror in her eyes and I held back. I let her go with one last blow on her nose.

"Get out of here. Next time you mess with us I'll kill you." I spat.

She glanced at me for the last time, and ran away with her tail between her legs.

"Thanks Dad." Hunter gasped. But I didn't have time to answer because the copper tom barreled into me again. I would've gone down if Hunter hadn't jumped in. Together, we drove him toward the bushes until he hissed and ran away to the ally where the calico cat had gone.

The black tom saw him leave and ran after him, tearing himself away from Shira. Shira was bleeding, and had many scratches on her face, but she hissed back at him.

Nico and Echo had been sitting back to back watching the fight. They had even dealt a few blows strategic themselves and still had the glow of battle in their eyes.

"That was amazing, Dad!" Echo mewed. "Can we do that again?"

"No!" I hissed, horrified. I realized they were kidding, and sighed. "Are you okay?" I asked without waiting for an answer as I shuffled painfully over to check on Shira.

"Your leg is bleeding again." She told me as I approached her, but she was smiling proudly. I looked into her eyes, relieved that she seemed okay, even happy.

"What are you so cheerful about?" I asked her. "We just about got ourselves killed."

She just smiled some more and limped forward, rubbing her whiskers against mine. "I fought off that tomcat on my own, even with this bad leg." She told me. "I haven't felt this good about myself for a long time."

I nodded understandingly, and actually, I was quite impressed myself now that she mentioned it. It had taken both me and Hunter to deal with the others, but Shira had won her battle on her own.

We took a few moments rubbing our cheeks together, just enjoying the moment.

"Eww." Echo wrinkled her face at us. "Don't be mushy."

I laughed and turned away, leading the family toward the stairs that went up onto Terrah's porch.

"It smells so nice!" Echo meowed when we got to the house. "I like this house already!"

I purred. "Wait 'till you get inside." I told them.

I hunched my legs to jump up to the windowsill. "Ow!" I yowled. My leg hurt, and I couldn't bend it well.

"Dad!" Nico hurried to my side and helped me stand up. "Are you okay?"

"Yeah." I grunted. "I guess so."

"Can you get in?" Shira asked me.

"I think so." I said. "You guys get in first."

Shira looked at me with concern, and then called the kittens. "Kids. Get in the house."

One by one, they jumped up through the window and got in. Every time I heard them say; "Whoa!" or "Cool!" I found myself beaming.

I tried to jump again, but I still couldn't make it. I growled in frustration. Just then, I heard a car pulling in. It was Terrah, and as soon as she had parked and gotten out of the car, she came toward me.

Meowing, I padded over to meet her. Terrah petted me gently and then noticed my leg. "Oh, my gosh!" She said. "Your leg!"

She scooped me up, and carried me to the door. She stopped when she opened the door. Shira and the kittens all sat there blinking at her.

"Hello!" Brave old Hunter meowed in greeting.

"Awwww." Terrah said warmly, and kneeled down to take a close look at my family. Shira hissed when she did, backing protectively away and giving her a menacing look.

"You're hurt too." Terrah told Shira, as she fluffed up her hackles and arched her back defensively.

Terrah looked over at me too. My leg missing its bandage and fresh blood dripping down onto the floor. "It was the neighbor cats again, wasn't it?" She sighed with a hint of anger in her voice. "Honestly, I don't know what's gotten into them."

I shambled across the floor and rubbed myself at Shira's body so Terrah could see that she was my wife, not an enemy.

Hunter ventured closer to Terrah, his nose twitching curiously and nervously while Echo and Nico hid behind me.

Terrah stretched her hand out to pet Hunter. He flinched at her first touch, hissing. "It's okay." I told him. "She won't hurt you."

Hunter relaxed at that, and didn't move when Terrah petted him again. Soon, he was purring and lying on his belly.

Echo and Nico padded closer too, and not long after, they were all rubbing themselves to get petted.

Shira glanced nervously around. I gave her a little push toward Terrah and she crouched down, growling. I couldn't know whether she was growling at me or Terrah.

"Here, let me get you some cat food. I bought some on the way home." Terrah said standing up. The kittens followed her meowing.

"So?" I prompted. "The kittens like it."

Shira glared at me. "I don't like this one bit."

"But you will soon." I said heading toward the kitchen at the sound of a cat food can opening.

Even Shira had to follow me toward the delicious smell of food. When we got there, the kittens were all munching vigorously. "Dad, we've got to stay here." Hunter said.

"Yes!" Echo added her mouth full of food. "Today's the best day ever!"

Shira padded over to them grooming their fur. Nervously, she settled next to them to eat a little. She was hungry and quickly became so engrossed in the food that she didn't notice Terrah petting her. But when she realized what Terrah was doing, she jumped back, bristling.

"It's okay." Terrah said, raising her hand and making a peace sign. "I meant you no harm."

Shira just stared at her warily and scooted over to my side. I licked her. "You'll get used to it." I told her.

"What do you mean I'll get used to it?" Shira snapped at me. "We didn't decide that we were going to stay here yet."

I shrugged and squeezed between Hunter and Nico to get more food. Shira took a spot as far away from Terrah as possible.

"We are going to stay here, right?" Hunter asked when we were done, sniffing around at a fluffy yellow blanket. Terrah had made a cozy nest stuffed with blankets just for us. Echo snuggled beside him.

I looked at Shira. "Well?" I pressed.

Shira looked back at me with a forceful stare. "I'm not a people cat." She told me harshly. "You can't just expect me to be okay in a place like this. I need some time, but I'll agree to stay here tonight for the sake of the family. We need a warm, safe place to relax. One night and that's all." With that, she turned away and stormed out of the kitchen.

I sighed as I watched her walk away. The rest of us stayed until the food was gone. After that, we all followed after Shira into the living room, and we looked around to find her. But she was not anywhere to be seen. "Hey. Where's mom?" Hunter asked, with a worried voice.

It was then that we heard a faint sound coming from the hallway. It sounded like a fish splashing weakly in the water. Hunter dashed in the direction of the sound with me hot on his heels, and Terrah following close behind in her bath gown.

The water sounds were coming from the bathroom, and I got there ahead of everyone else. The wall of the tub loomed above me, and I reared up, placing my forepaws on the slippery metal. I was just peering over as Terrah knelt down beside me, leaning over the bathtub and reaching inside. It was Shira.

Panic gripped my heart as I watched Terrah lift her limp body up, water dripping noisily back into the tub from her flattened fur. Terrah grabbed a huge towel that was hanging on the wall and wrapped Shira's limp body inside it, carrying her out of the bathroom. The whole family followed in a state of shocked disbelief.

But suddenly, just as Terrah was about to sit down on the sofa, we heard Shira cough weakly. Relief filled my mind at the sound, and I let a little bit of the tenseness drain out of my body.

All of us jumped up onto the sofa beside Terrah, and I sat there, licking Shira's muzzle as Terrah massaged her, pressing on her chest again and again. Finally, Shira heaved a huge lung full of water up, and it splashed on me and the towel. But the effort woke her up, and she looked at me weakly, coughing some more. She couldn't speak yet, and simply laid her head down on Terrah's lap, closing her eyes.

We all sat there like that, and listened as Shira's breathing slowly returned to normal. Gradually she fell into a deep, contented sleep. Shortly, we were all purring happily, and feeling quite relaxed.

My eyes were closed when I heard Shira softly say. "You were right. She *is* like Pete. Not all humans are bad. I'm sorry I was so harsh on you before."

I purred. "It's okay. I forgive you."

The days after that were wonderful. Shira and Terrah got so close. Shira even rolled on her belly and meowed to get stroked behind the ears. One rainy day, we were all gathered in the kitchen. Terrah was drinking hot chocolate, and I was sitting on her lap. Suddenly, Terrah jerked as if she remembered something.

"You know…" She said. "…I'm still amazed that you found me after all these years." A look of sadness clouded her face. "We tried to come back quickly." She was speaking quite softly now. "But we were on the expressway, and there was no place turn around. When we finally got back, we looked for you for hours, but we just couldn't find you." She looked at me, fluffing my cheek fur absently with her thumb. I saw a tear in her eye. "It was getting dark, and Dad said we had to go. He just…" Her voice trailed off sadly.

But it was nice for me to hear her. I had blamed her for so long, and now I could finally let all of that go. Terrah took a drink of her hot chocolate, and smiled. "I only ever had one cat." She told me. "But now, there are five of you, so I guess I should call you something other than Kitty."

I pricked up my ears in excitement and curiosity as she looked thoughtfully at me, tapping on her chin. "Seeker!" She said enthusiastically at last. "What do you think, boy?"

"I *love* it." I purred sincerely. I finally had a name to be proud of. It was a good name and a happy ending.

Epilogue

That summer was the best ever, and the first of many like it.

We drank milk and ate cat food and tuna to our heart's content. Sometimes, we would go out to the garden and catch mice or birds to eat. Terrah always left the window open so we could go in and out as we pleased.

We had some friends in the neighborhood. The pretentious Persian who had given us advice became Shira's friend, which surprised me because I thought they had nothing in common.

We visited our old friend Bruiser from time to time. He always greeted us with his big sloppy grin.

The kittens grew and grew until they were almost as big as me and Shira. Echo had kittens of her own, which she named; Branch, Twig, and Leaf. They were so cute, and they looked just like their mother. Amazingly, their father was the copper tom who had attacked us with his gang. So that was how we made peace with the neighborhood bullies. The copper cat, whose name was Flick, came to see his kittens from time to time.

Brave old Hunter got bored of house cat life and wanted adventures of his own. He left the house and became a loner cat. But he stayed in the area and sometimes came to visit us. Echo's kittens loved him because he always had great stories to tell.

Nico stayed with us and became fat and lazy, but we didn't mind.

Shira and I, we were a happy pair. We finally felt safe and comfortable. My name was Seeker, and I was the happiest cat in the whole wide world.

Annika Kim loves cats and has been an activist in behalf of stray or feral cats in her neighborhood. She is currently living in South Korea.

Jeff Rogers is an author and President of EECA (English Educator's Cooperative Association). He is also currently living in South Korea with his loving wife.

Collaborating on a book together is a challenge. We worked steadily for about a year to complete Seeker. But we survived to see our ideas in print.